BLOOD TIES IN CHEF VOLEUR

BY
MALLORY KANE

MILLS
BOON

® and ™ are trademarks owned and used by the trademark owner and/or its licensee. Trademarks marked with ® are registered with the United Kingdom Patent Office and/or the Office for Harmonisation in the Internal Market and in other countries.

Published in Great Britain 2014
by Mills & Boon, an imprint of Harlequin (UK) Limited,
Eton House, 18-24 Paradise Road, Richmond, Surrey, TW9 1SR

© 2014 Rickey R. Mallory

ISBN: 978-0-263-91368-2

46-0814

Harlequin (UK) Limited's policy is to use papers that are natural, renewable and recyclable products and made from wood grown in sustainable forests. The logging and manufacturing processes conform to the legal environmental regulations of the country of origin.

Printed and bound in Spain
by Blackprint CPI, Barcelona

Mallory Kane has two very good reasons for loving reading and writing. Her mother was a librarian, and taught her to love and respect books as a precious resource. Her father could hold listeners spellbound for hours with his stories. He was always her biggest fan.

She loves romantic suspense with dangerous heroes and dauntless heroines, and enjoys tossing in a bit of her medical knowledge for an extra dose of intrigue. After twenty-five books published, Mallory is still amazed and thrilled that she actually gets to make up stories for a living.

Mallory lives in Tennessee with her computer-genius husband and three exceptionally intelligent cats. She enjoys hearing from readers. You can write her at mallory@mallorykane.com.

For my family. Blood ties and love together are the strongest. Thank you all. I love you.

And for fans of The Delancey Dynasty.
Your loyalty and love for the Delanceys
overwhelms me. Thank you.

Chapter One

Jack Bush looked at his wife of one month as she lifted her arms above her head to slip on the exquisite pink dress. It slid down over her breasts, past her waist and hips, draping over her slender curves and porcelain skin, and flowed like a thick gleaming river past her ankles to puddle just slightly on the floor.

He tried to swallow but his throat was dry. He felt himself becoming aroused as her palms smoothed the satin. He stepped behind her and rested his hands on top of hers at the curve of her hips.

"Jack, I have to finish dressing."

"I know," he murmured as he kissed the little bump at the curve of her shoulder. He pushed the dainty strap away and slid his lips and tongue across to the curve of her neck, feeling triumphant when she took a long breath and angled her head to give him access.

"Isn't it fashionable to be late?" he asked.

"Not when the party's for us and it's at my mother's house."

"Ouch," he said. "Way to deflate the, um…enthusiasm."

Cara Lynn Delancey laughed and turned to him. She

slid the strap back up onto her shoulder, pushed her fingers through her hair and shook it out, then she pulled her dress up and hooked her thumbs over the elastic band of her silk bikini panties, pushed them down and kicked them off. "I'm ready," she said.

Jack stared at her open-mouthed. "You're not really… Really? At your mother's house?"

Her face was still creased with laughter, but two bright red spots stood out in her cheeks, revealing her embarrassment. "Haven't you been telling me I need to be less inhibited?"

He did his best to tamp down his desire by picturing her in baggy jeans and a stretched-out T-shirt, bent over her loom in her studio. That didn't help. She was sexy as hell in an oversize T-shirt, too.

He shook his head. "Okay. Let's go. But God help you if somebody steps on your dress, because those little straps will never hold up."

She shot him a worried look, then started toward the panties. Jack grabbed her hand. "We're late," he said with a meaningful look.

"Right," she said, sending a regretful glance back at the panties.

JACK COULDN'T BELIEVE his plan had worked. He was here, standing in the gigantic front hall of the Delancey family home, as an invited guest. No, he amended. Not as a guest—as *family*.

He'd done it. He'd married Cara Lynn Delancey, and now he was about to meet the majority of the Delancey family for the first time, all in one place. So far, he'd only met her parents, one of her brothers and a cousin since he'd eloped with Cara Lynn a month before.

Tonight, all the names in his grandfather's letters were about to be attached to real people, and one of those people held the answers he needed. Someone in this room knew what really happened the night Con Delancey was murdered twenty-eight years ago at his fishing cabin on Lake Pontchartrain.

Jack looked around, trying to appear worldly and unimpressed, while inside he felt like a kid at Christmas. He was here, finally, surrounded by the infamous politician's children and grandchildren. This was better than his wildest dream.

Cara Lynn appeared beside him, slipping her hand into his and squeezing. Gritting his teeth, he tried to keep his expression pleasant as he did his best to ignore the soft warmth of her fingers tightening around his in nervous anticipation.

That was the hardest part of being around Cara Lynn—maintaining the delicate balance between appearing to be the loving bridegroom, totally in love with his beautiful wife, and his true mission.

"Jack, remember I told you about my great-aunt Claire?"

Jack did remember. Claire Delancey was Con's sister. According to Jack's grandfather, Claire could be holding the single most important piece of information he needed—Lilibelle Guillame Delancey's last journal. "Your aunt that lives in France? Sure."

"Well," she paused and Jack saw her lips tremble.

"She had a stroke sometime yesterday, and during the night she died. Mama just told me."

Claire Delancey dead? Jack's brain whirled. How was that going to affect his plan? Had vital information about Con Delancey's death died with his sister?

Cara Lynn lifted a shaky hand to her mouth. He looked at her. Her eyes were dry, but the glow was gone from their blue depths. "Are you okay?" he asked. "I know you loved her a lot."

She smiled sadly. "I'm going to miss her horribly. She lived in France for my entire life, but I've spent summers over there since I was ten."

"She was your grandfather's sister?" he asked.

Cara Lynn nodded. "And my grandmother's best friend."

"Oh, yeah?" He remembered. That was why his grandfather was sure Claire had important information about Con's death.

Cara Lynn sighed and Jack put his arm around her and kissed her temple. "I'm sorry," he said. *For more than one reason.*

"There's Mama. She's waving at us. Come on. Maybe the press is here and we can get that part of the reception over with."

Jack looked across the room at Betty Delancey, who stood with one hand on the back of her husband Robert's wheelchair. Next to her was a thin, dour man in a business suit who held a gray metal lockbox. Jack figured he ought to have a chain and a handcuff, or, given how tightly he was holding the box, maybe he didn't. He started to ask Cara Lynn who the guy was and what was in the box, but she pointed toward the tall front doors.

"Look over there. Do you recognize the man and woman coming this way? They're the co-anchors of a local news show. They're here to interview us, take pictures and do a write-up of our *romantic* elopement and, of course, the large reception my family is giving us tonight."

"News show? Really?" Jack stopped cold in his tracks.

"What's wrong?" Cara Lynn asked teasingly. "Are you camera shy?"

The words *camera shy* didn't even begin to describe what Jack was feeling. *News show* meant cameras, and cameras meant exposure. Jack was nobody in comparison to the Delanceys, but he knew that because of who they were, he would be in the spotlight for a few hours or days until the next society story came along.

His mother was in Florida, and he'd worked and lived in Biloxi for the past nine years. With any luck, none of his friends there would pay much attention to a two minute segment of society news from the north shore of Lake Pontchartrain.

"Jack?"

"It's okay. I just don't like being thrust into the spotlight by surprise," he said. "I'll manage." He could tell his friends that he'd finally changed his name legally. They knew that he'd always wanted to get rid of the Francophied *Jacques*.

It took several minutes for the co-anchors to set the stage for the interview. Meanwhile, Jack saw the dour man with the box lean in a couple of times and whisper something to Cara Lynn's mother, triggering a shake of her head and a hand gesture that obviously meant something like *just hang in there. It won't be long now.*

"What's that box?" he finally asked Cara Lynn.

"I'm not sure, but it could be—"

A man in a baseball cap with the TV station's letters on it waved at them. The way he was throwing out orders and waving his arms, Jack figured he was probably the director. "Could you two get over here please," he said, motioning them toward him. He proceeded to get them positioned just right for the video and still shots, then introduced Jack and Cara Lynn to the co-anchors.

Despite the fact that they appeared to be slavering at the idea of sinking their teeth into the youngest Delancey grandchild, Cara Lynn was gracious and polite. Jack had learned that about her as soon as he'd met her. She was probably the most compassionate person he'd ever known. Her condolences were never disingenuous, her delight never false, her disappointment never exaggerated or tempered. With Cara Lynn, if she said it she meant it.

The entire filming was over within about five minutes. The only thing either of the co-anchors had asked Jack was what it felt like to be thrust into such a large and famous family. Jack had given an innocuous answer and smiled for the camera. Then he was dismissed and the spotlight was on Cara Lynn and her parents.

"Okay, people," the man in the baseball cap shouted. "That should do it." He turned to Cara Lynn's mother. "We've already taken long shots of the house, so we're out of here. I'll send you proofs and you can determine how many of each you might like to have for your personal remembrances."

All the photographers and engineers and crew headed for the doors. Cara Lynn's mother looked around. "Are we just family and friends now?" she asked the tall, good-looking man standing on the other side of Cara Lynn.

"I think so," the man said. He took advantage of his height and looked around the large open hall. Then he walked over to Jack. "I think you've probably met just about everybody else by now. I'm Lucas Delancey, Cara Lynn's oldest brother. I've been outside keeping an eye on the TV crew." He held out his hand.

Jack shook it. "I'm Jack Bush, but I'm betting you already know that."

Lucas smiled. "Well, I *am* a detective," he said. "Excuse me." Lucas walked over to the middle of the room and called out. "Hey, everybody. My mother has a presentation to make to our lovely little Cara Lynn. Everybody want to gather around?"

"Now what?" Jack whispered to Cara Lynn.

"I don't know. Nobody ever tells me anything. They spend all their time 'protecting' me." She emphasized the word with air quotes. "All I know is my mother was determined to have a reception for us since we, and I quote, 'deprived her of the North Shore wedding of the season.'"

"Really?"

Cara Lynn took his arm. "Of course. Don't you know how much havoc you created in the Delancey family by sweeping me away to a hurried justice of the peace wedding and no honeymoon and worst of all, no media coverage?"

"Then I guess I apologize."

"Don't apologize to me. Why do you think I agreed to elope? Save the apologies for my mother."

Jack watched as she, like everyone else in the room, turned toward Betty Delancey.

"Hello," Betty said from the front of the room. "I want to thank all of you for coming."

Jack tuned out most of what Betty said. Instead, he paid attention to the man with the lockbox, wondering when he was going to open the mysterious container, and of course, what was inside it. His grandfather had always talked about Lilibelle Guillame Delancey's last journal, the one she'd written in compulsively for hours and hours during the days following Con Delancey's death.

He heard Lilibelle's name and turned his attention back to what Betty was saying as she began to explain why Cara Lynn had been left a special inheritance from her grandmother, Lilibelle Guillame.

"She was the youngest child and the only grand-daughter," Betty said, "since at the time we all thought her dear cousin Rosemary was dead."

There were murmurs and whispers all around Jack. He couldn't, by any means, remember all the people he'd met tonight. After all, he knew that in addition to the eleven grandchildren and their spouses, there were other relatives and some close friends present.

Then her mother called Cara Lynn up to the front

and gave a short, sweet speech about what a joy it was to have her as a daughter, while at the same time managing to sneak in a small admonishment about her having eloped.

"Your grandmother died when you were twelve. She always said that part of the legacy of the Delanceys was that there were very few girls born to the family. She wanted to leave something very special to her granddaughters. Rosemary, of course, received the monogrammed Delancey silver service for twenty-four when she graduated from high school. And for you, Cara Lynn, she left you her journals. She wrote in them daily, starting when she was twelve years old. She also left you the contents of this box." Betty indicated the box.

The man holding the box set it carefully on the table near him and unlocked it.

"Come Cara, see what you have and show everyone."

Cara Lynn walked up and kissed her mother on the cheek. Then she stepped over to the metal box and lifted the lid—and gasped aloud.

The murmurs and whispers started up again as some of the crowd pushed closer, hoping to get a first glimpse of the contents. She reached inside and pulled out a beautiful, pale beige leather-bound journal. The cacophony of voices increased when she held it up.

Beside Jack, a tall thin man gasped and muttered something under his breath. Jack glanced at him, but his attention was glued to Cara Lynn, or more specifically, to the journal in her hand.

"What is it?" a voice chimed in.

"Is that one of Grandmother's journals?" another voice called.

Cara Lynn opened the book and looked at the first page. Her face brightened with delight. "It *is*. I have the full set, so this one *must* be the last journal she kept, from the year my grandfather died."

Jack's heart leapt into his throat and he remembered his grandfather's words. *On the day Con died, all she did was write in that book. The police were investigating the scene and questioning us and she just sat there and scribbled. She had to be writing down what happened. If I could just get my hands on that book, I know it contains the truth.*

Jack looked around him, but he garnered no information from the peoples' reactions. Everybody seemed mesmerized by the sight of the journal.

Betty walked over and stood beside her daughter. "But that's not all, dear, is it?"

Cara Lynn held the journal tucked under one arm and reached back into the box with her other hand. She pulled out something that was wrapped in what looked like an ancient, frayed piece of linen or cotton.

"Unwrap it, darling," her mother said, clasping her hands together in front of her, a look of unabashed anticipation and excitement on her face.

Jack held his breath just like a lot of other people in the room. He knew what Cara Lynn was holding.

"Mom, I'll hold it if you'll unwrap it," Cara Lynn said, apparently unwilling to let go of the journal. Betty carefully lifted each corner of the delicate-looking cloth and let it fall over Cara Lynn's hand. The slow reveal allowed the diamonds and rubies and sapphires and emeralds in the tiara to sparkle and shine to maximum effect.

Cara Lynn gasped, as did the entire room. Whether by accident or design, Betty had chosen the perfect place to reveal the tiara for the first time. They were standing under a huge crystal chandelier, which caught the reflections from the gems and turned them into thousands of multicolored sparks of light that danced across the walls and floor.

Cara Lynn turned the tiara so she could look at the large diamond in its center. The whispers and murmurs grew louder and louder until within a few seconds, the sound was deafening.

Jack himself was mesmerized, but not by the sparkly tiara, nor the journal under Cara Lynn's arm. He was caught by the open, unfettered joy on his wife's face.

"Oh," she said, clutching the journal more tightly and looking from the tiara out over the crowd of people, 80 percent of whom were related to her. "I...can barely speak," she said breathlessly, her gaze sweeping across the faces until she met Jack's. The smile that shone on her face made him want to cry. "I've never been so happy as I am right now."

Jack blinked and averted his gaze. It was like walking on hot coals to look into her eyes and hear her talking about her happiness. He turned away and found himself toe-to-toe with a tall, fit man in his late forties. Jack took a better look at him. His hair was dyed black, which made him look more like a cartoon than a real person, because nobody's hair was that black naturally. His eyes were dark brown, and right now they were fixed on Jack.

"You're Jack, Cara Lynn's husband," he said firmly, as if he was worried that Jack didn't know. "And your last name is…?" He embellished his unfinished question with a flourishing gesture.

"Bush," Jack responded, offering a small smile to counteract his flat response. Then with a wider smile he said, "Jack Bush."

"Bush," the man said thoughtfully.

"And you are?" Jack asked, resisting an almost overwhelming urge to run his finger along the inside of his collar. The way the man said his name made Jack second-guess his decision to take the name Bush. These people were as much—maybe more—old New Orleans as his family. Any one of them might know enough French to make the connection. Broussard was from a French word meaning *brush man* or *bushman*. At the time, he'd thought he was being clever. Now he wished he'd chosen Smith or Johnson.

He looked back at the man and waited for him to introduce himself. Finally, after shooting his cuffs and smoothing his school tie with a hand weighted down by a large Austrian crystal-studded ring, the black-haired man lifted his nose slightly. "Paul Guillame."

The name sent a streak of adrenaline through Jack. *Paul Guillame. A cheating, lying skunk who helped Con's wife frame me for murder,* Granddad had written about him. *Watch your back.* Jack kept his expression neutral and waited, but Guillame did not offer his hand, so Jack didn't, either. "You're related to the Delanceys?" he asked innocently.

Paul straightened and looked down his nose at him. "Senator Delancey's wife was a Guillame," he said. "The Guillames are a very old family here. But you, Jack Bush." The man gestured around vaguely. "I hope you realize that you have committed a serious crime against the Delanceys and that they are even now preparing your punishment."

Jack looked at him, stunned into silence. *Crime? Punishment?* What was the man talking about?

Guillame leaned forward. "Are you satisfied that the crime was worth whatever punishment will be meted out? Can your love for our pretty little youngest survive the wrath of the Delanceys?"

So that was it. His *crime* against the Delanceys was stealing their youngest. His paralyzed vocal chords loosened. "Sometimes something is so beautiful that it must be had, at any cost or any punishment."

Again, as he'd hoped to do when they first came in, he tried to sound worldly, but he wasn't sure if he'd pulled it off or if he'd just sounded silly.

Paul Guillame smiled. He reminded Jack of the Cheshire Cat in *Alice in Wonderland*. "Be aware, young Mr. Bush, our Cara Lynn has four brothers and four cousins. That's eight descendants of Con Delancey. So anyone who hurts her faces death times eight." Paul raised a hand with an impeccable manicure and pointed a finger at him. "Now, Monsieur Jacques, you add your sword to the pledge, which makes it death times nine."

All the blood rushed from Jack's head at Guillame's

use of the French pronunciation of his name. For a split
second he felt as though he might pass out. But he kept
himself composed and managed not to look around to
see if anyone had noticed Paul calling him *Jacques*. He
hoped his hand was not visibly shaking as he placed it
over his heart. "I so pledge, *Monsieur*." He sketched a
little bow. When he raised his gaze to meet Guillame's,
the man's black eyes were on the box again, but only for
a brief instant, then he turned back to Jack.

"So, tell me Jack, where are you from anyway?"

As a Southerner, Jack understood the question. When
asked *where are you from,* a Southerner knows the asker
is not interested in where you live, or even where you
grew up, He wants you to lay out your family's history
as far back as you know it.

Jack had prepared for this question and his brain was
already queuing up the background he'd invented for
himself. "My family originally came from—"

The room went dark. Pitch dark.

Startled, Jack took a second to orient himself.
Screams and yells came from all around him. Someone tall bumped against him in the dark and almost
knocked him off balance. He righted himself, reaching
around him for something, anything, to grab in order to
break his fall. His fingers brushed a sleeve. The sleeve
was pulled away immediately, but Jack noticed that the
person who'd bumped into him had been tall—at least
as tall as he, and wearing a suit jacket or sports coat.
The material that had brushed against his fingers was a
thick, heavier fabric, the kind used to make men's coats.

Then Jack heard a sound that penetrated all the other

sounds around him. It was a shriek and a cry of pain. *Cara Lynn*.

At that instant the lights came back on. Jack, who was standing less than six feet from where Cara Lynn had been holding up the bejeweled tiara, saw her, crumpled on the floor in her satin gown, not moving.

"Cara!" he cried, just as someone, maybe Cara's mother, screamed. "Oh, my God, Cara Lynn!" From another part of the room someone cried out, "The tiara! It's gone!"

People were milling around everywhere. Jack saw the Delancey men moving in concert, as if they were all part of one company or battalion. In sync, they divided up. Some headed toward Cara Lynn and her mother. Some headed for the front doors. One of them—it looked like one of the twins—pulled out his cell phone, calling the St. Tammany Parish Sheriff's Office, no doubt.

When Jack got to Cara Lynn, two of her brothers were already there, bending over her, and a third Delancey was running toward them. He heard someone shout, "There he goes. Out the side door!" Jack leapt up onto a chair and spotted a man dressed in black, hurrying toward a pair of French doors on the side of the large hall. The man glanced backward, then threw open the doors and bolted. He was cradling something close to his chest like a football. Jack couldn't tell what it was.

Around the doors, people were crying out and pointing, and Jack saw Delancey men pushing their way through the crowd, but the man in black obviously had a huge head start.

Jack's muscles tensed and his tendons tightened, although intellectually, he knew that if the Delanceys—cops, military men and investigators—couldn't catch the thief, he had no chance. But just at the instant when he was about to spring down off the chair and try to lend his help, he heard Cara Lynn's voice.

"Jack?"

It was raspy and choked, but it was her. He turned back toward her. She had three of her big, capable Delancey protectors hovering over her, but she wasn't paying any attention to them. She was looking straight at him. Horrified, he saw blood streaming down the side of her face and her expression was twisted in pain.

"Cara?" he whispered. Then his gaze rose to the table where the journal and the tiara had sat. All that remained was the square of old cloth. The bejeweled crown and the book were gone. Jack cared nothing—less than nothing—for the tiara. But that journal, if it really was Lilibelle Guillame's last journal, could exonerate his grandfather from any wrongdoing, if his grandfather's theory was true and Lilibelle was the one who'd killed Con Delancey.

Jack glanced in the direction of the French doors. Then he looked at his wife, whom he'd duped into marrying him so he could find *that journal*.

He took a deep breath. *The journal!* his brain screamed. *Get the journal*. But his head didn't stand a chance against his stupid heart. Berating himself, he rushed to his bride's side, bent down and used his thumb to wipe blood away from the small ridge just above her brow. Instantly, the three men turned on him.

"Don't touch her," one said.

Before Jack could react, the second one, who'd been talking on the phone, said, "We've got cars coming from everywhere. That guy won't get far."

"Right. Lucas took off after him. He'll have him in handcuffs before the cruisers even get here," the third one said.

Before he finished speaking, someone in the direction of the French doors shouted. "Look! He dropped the tiara! See it—"

"Nobody move!" a voice boomed. "Hey! Pipe down! Barton, get that crown! Everybody—Shut! Up!"

"Did you see anything?" one of the brothers asked Cara Lynn as another pressed a handkerchief to the cut on her forehead.

"Has anybody got any water?" the third man shouted.

To Jack, their voices sounded like a swarm of bees around his head. It occurred to him that this was what Cara Lynn had been talking about when she'd described how she'd spent her life being suffocated by her brothers. He wanted to swat them away and take care of her himself. She might be their sister, but she was his wife.

Then he noticed that one of the straps of her gown was broken. And sure enough, just as he'd predicted, without the strap, the entire left side of the dress was quickly headed south, toward a serious wardrobe malfunction. Jack shrugged out of his jacket and placed it around her shoulders. She looked up at him gratefully and pulled the lapels of the coat closed and stuck her arms into the sleeves.

Her brothers glared at him but didn't say anything, so Jack stayed there with his arm around her.

By the time everybody was convinced that Cara Lynn was fine mentally, emotionally and physically, and no ambulance needed to be called, Lucas was back.

Everybody turned to look at him. Even Jack could read his expression like a children's book. No luck.

"He disappeared," Lucas said, a disgusted frown on his face.

"Oh, my God," Paul said from behind Jack. "Did he really drop the tiara?"

Lucas leveled a grim glare at Paul. "We recovered the tiara, but he got the journal. Did any of you get a look at his face? Cara Lynn?"

Beside Jack, Cara Lynn shook her head.

Lucas pushed the fingers of one hand through his hair, then shouted at no one in particular. "How in hell did he get in and grab that stuff in the middle of a room full of cops?"

Chapter Two

It was after midnight by the time Jack and Cara Lynn got home.

"You'd think with so many Delancey cops there as witnesses, it shouldn't have taken so long," Cara Lynn said, looking in her compact mirror at the cut on her forehead.

"Really?" Jack said. "It's only been three hours. My guess is if a thief had broken in and tried to steal a six or seven-figure piece of jewelry from any other house in this entire town, every single person there would have been hauled down to the police station, and many of them would still be there twenty-four hours later."

"Well, that's what they ought to do. It's stupid that nobody caught that thief." She gingerly touched the cut with her fingertip.

"I need to get you some antibiotic ointment and a strip bandage," Jack said.

"I'll do it. Damn, it still hurts."

"Why don't you get in bed and I'll get you some water or something?"

"I won't be able to sleep," she said.

Jack got a bottle of water out of the refrigerator, opened it and handed it to her. "Were you able to see anything? Could you tell anything about the thief?"

"See anything? I don't know what room you were in," she retorted, "but where I was it was black as pitch. Like I told the detective, I felt a hand on me, then I was pushed down and I hit my shoulder and head on the marble table. The next thing I knew everybody was hovering over me." She shivered.

"I think you need to go to bed," he said. "Don't you have to finish getting ready for your new show down in New Orleans in the morning?"

"Yes," she said. "I've still got one piece to finish. I should get up at five."

Jack grabbed a bottle of water for himself. He twisted the top off and took a long swallow, then gazed at her as if he was thinking about what he was going to say. "What do you think that tiara is worth?"

Cara Lynn shrugged and winced. "Damn it, my shoulder is sore, too. The tiara? I don't know. My grandmother said it was priceless, but she let me play Princess with it."

Jack paused with the bottle halfway to his lips. "You're kidding."

"No. I played dress-up with some of her old clothes and the tiara. I remember it was heavy. She got mad if I dropped it."

"I'll bet she did."

"I heard my parents and Uncle Michael talking about it once. They were saying half a million."

Jack's jaw tightened and the expression on his face

was unreadable, but it bothered her. "That guy was small-time. I don't get why he chanced stealing the tiara."

"What do you mean? If he'd gotten out of there, he'd be rich for the rest of his life."

He gave a half shrug. "How can anyone possibly sell something that famous?"

"He could remove the stones and sell them, right?"

"Those gigantic rubies and emeralds and diamonds have been photographed, measured, weighed. I'll guarantee you, the insurance company has an exact description of each stone. Whoever steals that baby better enjoy playing dress-up, because they're not going to get any money for it."

Cara Lynn stared at him. "You know an awful lot about famous jewels," she said. "Please tell me you're not an international jewel thief."

The corner of his mouth quirked up. "I'm not an international jewel thief. Every bit of that information can be found on the internet or in movies. *The Thomas Crown Affair,* for instance."

She nodded, but a trace of unease began to stir under her breastbone. It was the same feeling that had been a part of her ever since she and Jack had gotten married. She loved him and she was sure he loved her, but occasionally, he'd send her a look or make a comment that worried her.

There was something wrong between them and she couldn't figure out what it was. And every time she tried to talk to Jack about it, she ended up in his arms, making love.

"Come on," he said. "Let's go to bed. You need to get as much sleep as possible. I'll guarantee you're going to be sore tomorrow, and you'll probably have at least one bruise." He headed toward the bedroom.

"Okay. I'm just going to get the coffee ready to turn on in the morning."

Alone for the first time since the party had started, Cara Lynn stood in the middle of the kitchen floor while tears slid down her cheeks. She'd done her best not to cry in front of her brothers or Jack, but everything that had happened had built up in her until she could no longer hold back.

From the instant she'd managed to clear her head after hitting it against the marble table, she'd called for Jack. When the lights came back on, she'd spotted him standing on a chair, looking over the crowd toward the French doors, in the direction the thief had run.

As soon as he'd heard her call, he'd turned around. He'd looked horrified at the blood on her face, but before he'd rushed to her side, he'd glanced back toward the French doors one more time.

She'd sensed the struggle in him, and she'd found it odd. He wasn't like her brothers. Two cops, a former special forces officer and an attorney. She'd expected them to jump into action and they had. It was their training.

But Jack was an architect—and her husband. Why had his first thought been to pursue the thief rather than rush to her side to be sure she was okay?

Glancing cautiously toward her bedroom, she listened. She didn't hear anything. However, if Jack was true to form, he'd be back in the kitchen in a few minutes to get some more water before turning in.

She opened her clutch and looked inside. Then she breathed a sigh of relief. She'd been afraid she'd imagined slipping the old envelope out from between the pages of the journal and sliding it into her clutch when the lights had gone out.

Touching the slightly yellowing paper, she wondered if anyone else had noticed its corner sticking out between two pages of the journal. She didn't think so. When she' d lifted the journal out of the box she'd instinctively covered the corner with her fingers.

She wasn't sure why her first instinct had been to keep its existence secret. She just knew she felt compelled to do so.

Then the lights had gone out and someone jerked the journal out of her hand. She'd held onto the envelope and her clutch with all her strength as a pair of rough hands pushed her down. She'd stumbled, hit her head and almost passed out, but she hadn't let go of the envelope. Just as she was slipping it into her clutch, the emergency generator had growled and the lights had come back on. She was pretty sure no one had seen her.

She should have given it to the police. She should have told her brothers. But for some reason, with the journal gone, she felt as though this letter was hers. Hers and nobody else's. Not that she knew why she felt that way, or had any inkling of what was inside it.

She was looking at the back, with its sealed but crumbling flap. She turned it over and her heart gave a little leap. There was her name, written in the distinctive and utterly beautiful, yet almost impossible to decipher, lovely handwriting of her grandmother, Lilibelle Guillame. *For Cara Lynn.*

Most likely it was a sweet and rambling message about the sentimental meaning of the tiara and her journal. No matter what it was, she wanted to keep it secret at least until she had time to read it thoroughly. Right now, there was no time to look at it without the chance of Jack coming in.

So she went into the pantry and pulled on a loose baseboard underneath the bottom shelf. She tucked the envelope into the hollow space behind it, where she kept two thousand dollars in small bills, her passport and the beautiful emerald necklace her mother had given her when she graduated from college. The necklace had belonged to Betty's mother, who had been a diplomat's wife and traveled all over Europe with her husband. Just as she was replacing the baseboard, she heard Jack's bare feet coming down the hall.

Quickly, she got the baseboard into place, grabbed three bottles of water, then stepped out of the pantry into the kitchen.

Jack was opening the refrigerator, his bare toes sticking out from his dress pants. He'd removed his jacket and tie and unbuttoned his shirt. It hung open, revealing a hint of his excellent abs.

"What are you doing?" he asked.

"Putting some more water in the fridge," she said, wishing she'd grabbed something else. She'd restocked the water just that morning.

"Sparkling water? What for?" he asked, gesturing

toward the top shelf of the fridge. "There are—" he stopped. "There were three regular and three sparkling waters in here this morning. Now there's only two sparkling, counting this one." He held up the one he'd just picked up. "I thought you were gone all day."

"I was," she said, putting the three bottles on the shelf. "I was in a hurry so I didn't stop to get one. You must have drunk another one."

"Nope." He closed the door. "That's odd."

Cara Lynn thought about that morning. She'd rushed out so quickly she hadn't grabbed her usual bottle of water. "Well, if you didn't drink it and I didn't drink it—"

"What? You think someone came in here and drank our water?" he asked, his mouth quirked slightly. "Who's got keys?"

"Nobody, except the woman who cleans, and she had foot surgery three weeks ago."

Jack twisted the top off the water and took a long drink. "Maybe she came by."

"If she did, it was just for the water, because she certainly didn't clean," Cara Lynn said wryly.

"How can you tell?" Jack retorted.

She swatted at him and smiled. "Hilarious," she said, "considering I picked up four empty bottles just like this from your side of the bed this morning. I've got a long day tomorrow and I *will* take some water with me."

He didn't comment, just headed back to the bedroom. She added two more bottles to the refrigerator, then followed him, going into their bathroom to undress. She shrugged out of Jack's jacket, then dropped the single intact strap off her shoulder and let the dress fall to the floor, leaving her completely naked. She looked down at herself, blushing. She'd forgotten her little flirtation with her husband from before the party. He probably had, too.

Quickly, she reached for her blue silk nightgown and slipped it over her head. They were married, but that didn't change the fact that she'd only known Jack for two months. She hadn't quite gotten over her shyness yet.

"So, what did you think?" she asked Jack, peering around the bathroom door. He was in profile to her, unzipping his pants. His shirt was already off and the sight of his lean, tanned body made heat curl deep inside her, as it did every time she looked at him. He was the most beautiful man she'd ever seen. It was still hard for her to believe that they'd fallen in love at first sight. Actually, to be truthful, she wasn't surprised that she'd fallen for him. What amazed her was that he'd fallen in love with her so fast.

She wondered, as she had many times, had he felt the same startling ache in the middle of his chest that she had when they'd seen each other across the gallery floor where she was exhibiting her fiber-art pieces? Had he immediately felt desire like a tuning fork shimmering and humming inside him? Did he remember each and every second of that first glance, as she had? She would never forget how he'd met her gaze, his mouth curved in a secret smile she hadn't seen since, then walked straight over to her and asked her to skip the show and go with him to get something to eat.

Even though she'd been a headliner at the gallery that night, she'd gone with him. Four weeks later, they were married.

"Jack?" she said again.

"Hmm?" He glanced at her sidelong, his dark brows shadowing his eyes. "What did I think about what?"

"About all the Delanceys?"

"Oh. They're pretty intense, especially about the baby of the family. Even Paul Guillame got a dig in to me. He told me that your brothers and cousins had pledged *death times eight* to anyone who dared to harm you."

"Oh, you met Paul. Did he really say that? I can't believe it."

"Why?"

She shrugged, thinking about her distant cousin on her mother's side. "He doesn't seem that deep or that interested in anyone but himself."

"Whoa. Ouch. Catty much?"

She felt her cheeks turn pink. "That wasn't very nice, was it?"

Jack shook his head. "Nope. He might be shallow, but he's right about your brothers—and cousins. I bent down to check on you and three big guys were all over me like it was their job to take care of you, not mine."

Cara Lynn felt a warm glow start in her midsection. "You think it's your job to take care of me?"

He looked up, his brows knitted, as if he hadn't even thought about what he'd said. With a slight tilt of his head, he said, "I guess."

Cara Lynn laughed. "I really like that. Not that I need taking care of."

He smiled. "I know. You're perfectly capable of handling yourself."

"Please, tell my brothers that."

"Why? What's the problem with being doted on by your brothers?"

"Nothing, if all you get are the perks. But with four older brothers, I have to put up with the downside, too."

"Right. Please, tell me the downside to being the favorite in a huge family of wealthy Louisianans."

"Just like tonight. Nobody thinks I can take care of myself. They don't even think I can think for myself. It's like I've had five dads threatening boyfriends and checking what time I got home from dates my whole life. And if that's not enough, two of my brothers and three of my cousins are cops. I can't count how many times they've stopped my car on the road with blue lights blazing, just to be sure I'm all right and on my way home."

Jack laughed. "Nobody's threatened or stopped me."

She rolled her eyes. "You're hardly a *boyfriend*. But I can tell you this. If we hadn't eloped, we'd only be about a fourth of the way to the wedding by now."

Jack's grin faded and he looked at her closely. "Did you want a big wedding?" he asked.

"No," she said immediately. "I mean, sure I did, when I was a little girl, I dreamed about the huge wedding with the most beautiful white dress in the world and my knight in shining armor waiting at the end of the aisle. But what I found out as I got older is that the press and everybody who either loved or hated my grandfather, consider the Delanceys as *Louisiana royalty*." She pantomimed air quotes around the two words.

"So, your wedding would have been the event of the season?" He spoke lightly, but his jaw ticced, as it did occasionally when he couldn't relax the tension in it.

"Not that our family hasn't had quite a few weddings in the past few years, but yes. Especially since I was the last holdout *and* the only girl."

"What about your cousin Rosemary?"

"Rosemary and Dixon had the tiniest, least announced ceremony in the history of the state. And Hannah, Claire's granddaughter, and her fiancé, Mack, aren't planning on getting married until after her mom's liver transplant. So that left me as the only girl with even a chance at a big wedding." She gave a little sigh. "My mother has expressed her *extreme* disappointment that I denied her all the pomp and circumstance."

"We could still—" Jack started to say as he took off his pants and boxers.

Cara Lynn broke in. "Don't even go there," she commanded, unable to take her eyes off him. "Although, it would shut my family up. I can't tell you how much ribbing I've taken about being the last one to marry." She shook her head. "My brothers and cousins have been falling like dominoes over the past few years."

"So, when your cousin Paul said I was a criminal that needed punishment—?"

"He said that?"

"Yep. That's fine though," he said, hanging up his

dress pants and pulling on pajama bottoms. He looked at her and smiled.

She hated that false smile that said, *I'm smiling and agreeable, because that's what you want.* It had only appeared after they'd gotten married. In fact, she was pretty sure she could trace it back to the day—or at least within a few days—of their elopement.

"I'm glad they're worried about you," he finished.

Was he? He'd been so sweet and sexy and fascinating before they'd eloped. Now he was still sexy and fascinating, but he'd become more reserved and often seemed distant. The change in him made her nervous. It seemed as if sometimes, when he wasn't aware she was watching him, he appeared to be sad or even angry about something. Could it be he regretted marrying her?

She smiled back, feeling as if her smile was as vacant and false as his, and a shudder slid through her, as if a goose had walked over her grave.

Ignoring the sinking feeling in her chest each time she saw that artificial smile, she took a deep breath and walked out of the bathroom toward him. Jack, his pajama bottoms hanging loose and low on his hips, met her halfway.

"You are beautiful tonight," he said, running his palms down her bare arms and bending to kiss her shoulder. "Your skin glows like rose petals in moonlight."

"Wow," she said nervously, as his hands and lips began to stir her. "That's quite poetic."

"I have my moments," he murmured, tracing his fingertips along her shoulder where he had kissed, then up the side of her neck to her jaw, and farther, until he reached her eyebrow. He kissed her there. "Did you get a chance to look inside the book?" he asked softly.

"What?" The question surprised her. Usually, when he made love to her he was single-minded, focused, as if he were a surgeon performing a very delicate procedure that could be disastrous if he made one tiny mistake.

"Your inheritance from your grandmother. It was one of her journals, like the ones in your office, right?"

"Oh. The journal. It looked exactly like the others. They must be hugely expensive, with all that leather and engraving and lace and the metal page corners. But no. I started to open the cover to look at the first page, but the lights went out before I saw anything."

He pushed her hair away from her ear and nibbled on the earlobe. As she gasped with surprise and pleasure, he said, "What did the cover say?"

The front cover of each journal was engraved. She had traced the first line with her finger. "They all have her name at the top. When she was a little girl it just said Lilibelle Guillame. The later ones say Lilibelle Guillame Delancey. Beneath her name is the year. And the one that was snatched tonight had 1986 on it, I'm pretty sure."

"1986? Isn't that when Con Delancey died? I heard someone ask if it was her last journal. Was it?" he murmured.

Cara Lynn pushed away. "Why are you so interested in—"

He nipped at her earlobe, then lowered his head and

kissed her collarbone as his hand slid down, down, to catch the hem of her nightgown and push it up.

He ran his hand along her hip, then gasped. "I'd forgotten you took off your panties," he whispered as he caressed the delicate, sensitive skin on the inside of her thighs, then touched her intimately. He pressed his lips to the soft skin below her jaw and moaned as he increased the rhythm of his caresses.

At that instant, all rational thought left her head. Instead of trying to recapture even one of those thoughts, she slid her fingers into his hair, bending forward to reach for his mouth with hers.

He turned his head so that her kiss landed on his cheek, because he was bending toward her ear again. He nipped at it, a bit harder this time. At the same time, he whispered, "Beautiful."

Intense, nearly painful thrills spiraled through her. Her head fell back, exposing her neck and the underside of her chin to more caresses, but he stopped, pulling away. His long fingers hooked the straps of her nightgown and slid them over her shoulders. The loose, slippery silk fell to the floor, leaving her naked. She shivered, feeling her breasts tighten in anticipation of his touch.

He slid his palms down her arms to her elbows and farther, down to her fingers. Slipping past them, he cupped her firm bottom.

On the way back up her legs, thighs and hips, he skimmed his fingers along a path of exploration that turned every fraction of an inch of her body into an erogenous zone. Finally, when she was sure her wobbly knees wouldn't hold her up for another second, he cupped her breasts, barely large enough to fill his palms, and caressed the soft skin with his thumbs, moving closer and closer to the areolae.

With each caress, her breaths became quicker until the moment when the pads of his thumbs slid across the taut tips of her nipples. She gasped and moaned, and he bent his head to place his mouth on one hard point. He grazed it with his teeth. She arched her back and pushed her fingers into his hair, holding his head there, until he moved to the other breast to graze it and send flames arcing through her again.

"Jack, please," she begged, tightening her fists in his silky dark hair.

He raised his head and his dark, fathomless gaze met hers. "What?" he asked gruffly.

She knew this game. They played it often. She wanted him deeply, primally. He'd brought her to this point and he knew it. Now he wanted her to tell him what she wanted.

Only what she always said and what she really wanted were two entirely different things.

"Please, Jack, don't make me say it," she whispered.

He held her gaze, that little place in his jaw tensing and relaxing, tensing and relaxing. "Say it, Cara," he rasped. "Say it."

Tears burned in the back of her throat and she swallowed, hoping to keep the need to cry there and not allow it to crawl all the way into her eyes where they would fall and he would win. Her new husband, whom she did not know at all, but whose touch she craved like she craved air, would win again.

"Jack…"

His eyes left hers and moved down to her mouth. She saw his gaze slide over her face and down to her lips. She almost went over the edge just in anticipation of him kissing her. Because he rarely did.

She looked at his straight, hard mouth. Then she reached for it with hers. He stayed still and let her kiss him, but he barely reciprocated. Then, after a very few seconds, he pulled away and picked her up and tossed her onto the bed. He pushed his pajama bottoms down and off, then lay beside her and began to caress her intimately.

She gasped at the feel of his hand, his fingers, as he bent his head again to taste and tease her nipples. He lifted his head and looked at her. "Say it," he demanded.

Cara Lynn's throat spasmed and the tears escaped. They rushed to her eyes and gathered there, dampening her lids and seeping out to trickle across her skin and wet the pillowcase. She squeezed her lids shut, trying to wring out the last tear, then she opened them again and looked into Jack's shadowed ones.

"I want you inside me," she said. "I want you now."

He rose above her, the lean muscles of his arms and chest bulging with effort, and entered her with a shuddering breath. And then, what Cara Lynn really wanted, he finally gave her. Once he was inside her and filling her with his hot hard sex, he kissed her, just as deeply and intimately as she had not dared to ask him to. It would crush her if he ever refused.

As the quest for release built until she thought she would burst, and as he thrust harder and harder until she was sure she couldn't stand it, his kiss also deepened, until she felt close to passing out from the sheer flood of pleasure and love and lust that overwhelmed her.

Then she did burst into ecstasy and Jack burst with her. For a brief moment out of time they were two supernovas crashing in the depths of space, becoming one, a pure blue flame of energy and love, and nothing else mattered.

Afterward, Jack lay there as long as he could, holding Cara Lynn. Her head fit perfectly in the hollow of his shoulder and her quiet breaths warmed the soft skin beneath his jaw line. Her slender, supple body molded perfectly to his. He hated that.

He shifted restlessly and she made a soft sound in her throat. "It's okay. Go back to sleep," he said, as he always did, then he slid his arm out from under her and rolled up off the bed.

He pulled on his pajama bottoms and went into the living room and through the French doors out onto the balcony. The night was cool and a breeze blew in off the Mississippi River. The sky was pale with the lights from the cruise ships and the fishing boats. Jack closed his eyes and took a long breath, reminding himself why he was standing here, in this place, with the taste and scent of Cara Lynn Delancey—Cara Lynn Bush—still in his mouth and nose.

All for show. "All for show," he said aloud, wishing he could shout it. Wishing he could tattoo it on the inside of his eyelids. And wishing, just for an instant, that he was not Jacques Broussard, grandson of the man who died in prison, falsely accused of the murder of Con Delancey, but merely a stranger.

Then, as happened when he let his guard down, he thought about what might have been, had he met Cara Lynn accidentally, if they'd had a chance to meet and learn to know each other in a world apart from reality—

The sound of the French doors opening stopped that thought cold.

"Hey." Cara Lynn's soft voice wrapped around his sore heart like a velvet bag that protects a fragile crystal. "Are you okay?"

"Sure," he responded. "Just wanted some air. I got hot."

She stepped out onto the balcony beside him. "It's cool out here, isn't it? Look at the river. It's so beautiful at night."

"Really? You like all the garish lights on the cruise ships and the bridges? They're just light pollution."

She slapped at his arm playfully. "No, they're not. It's like Christmas every night!" she cried. "They blink and twinkle just like Christmas Eve when you're supposed to be in bed. I love it. And after it rains, the whole horizon turns into a wonderland, shining like thousands of sparklers."

He looked at her, his mouth curving upward in a reluctant smile. "How did you get to be twenty-six years old without ever growing up?" he asked. "You're like a child. Does nothing bad ever touch you? Do you never feel sad or angry or grief-stricken?"

To his chagrin, her smile faded and the sparks in

her eyes went out. "Of course bad things happen, Jack. Of course I can be sad and angry and grief-stricken. I thought my heart would break when my best friend Kate's little boy was kidnapped recently." She stared out beyond him, into an unhappy distance.

After a long time, she looked back at him and her smile returned. "But he was fine, and then I met you and my world was happy again." She threw her arms up. "And it's a beautiful night. Want to sleep out here? I can make a pallet on the balcony floor out of quilts."

Jack shook his head. "I need to work on some plans. You need to go to sleep. Don't forget everything you have to do tomorrow."

Cara Lynn nodded and kissed him on the nose.

He recoiled. He didn't mean to. But it was a knee-jerk reaction to the closeness he felt whenever they kissed. The longing that simmered deep inside him was becoming harder and harder to control. He craved her kiss and yet he didn't like kissing her, because he was convinced that it was the kissing and touching that were the most intimate acts, not the sex.

This balancing act he was performing was about to drive him crazy. He didn't want her to get even the most fleeting thought that he might not love her. But at the same time, he was becoming desperate to protect himself from falling for her. He had to keep all his plates spinning in the air, because through her was the only way he was ever going to find the proof he needed to clear his grandfather's name.

So he returned her casual kiss—pressing his lips to her cheek near her temple.

She stepped back, her eyes bright. "Actually, yes," she said, obviously working to make her tone casual and talkative. "I do have a lot to do tomorrow, and I'm tired tonight, for some reason." She smiled at him as she backed through the French doors. "G'night, handsome."

"Good night, beautiful," he muttered, but she'd already gone inside and closed the doors.

Chapter Three

Jack stayed on the balcony for another fifteen minutes or so, staring at the bridge lights. He squinted to see if that would help him to see them as Christmas lights, but it was a waste of time. Lights were lights, not fairy tale sparkles or holiday decorations.

However, they did draw the eye, kind of like a river full of stars. For a while he stared at them, letting his thoughts wander back over the party. He'd tried to catalog each person's name as he met them, equating them to what his granddad had said about them, as best he could remember. And while he did that, he worked on remembering who he might have seen that didn't seem to belong.

Cara Lynn's father, Robert, was a wheelchair-bound man who had difficulty speaking. His grandfather had told him about the older of Con Delancey's two sons, both of whom had been young men with new families when Granddad had known them twenty-eight years ago. He'd called Robert angry and bitter, incapable of holding his whiskey or his temper.

It hurt Jack to think that Cara Lynn had been brought

up in such an angry, hostile home. But from her accounting, her experience had been very different than her older brothers'.

Harte and I didn't have the same father as Lucas, Ethan and Travis, she'd told him. *By the time we were old enough to remember, he'd had the stroke. The only anger I remember was toward himself—his body. Trouble talking and walking.*

He thought about his own parents and how he had grown up. As an only child, the problems he'd had with his folks stemmed from their over-protectiveness of him. Their biggest fear for him was that he spent too much time at the federal penitentiary visiting his granddad. But they had never refused to let him go.

Michael, Con's youngest son, seemed like a paragon of normalcy compared to Robert. Jack knew from Cara Lynn about Michael's time spent in prison, as well as his issues with his oldest son Dawson, but he seemed a likeable man, and his children seemed extraordinary.

In fact, it was a little disgusting just how likeable, intelligent and successful all the Delancey grandchildren were.

Jack wondered how they would react when they found out that Armand Broussard, who'd spent over twenty-five years in prison for their grandfather's murder, was innocent. Jack wasn't sure who had actually killed Con Delancey, but he knew his granddad hadn't done it.

He glanced absently in the direction of the foyer, where his briefcase sat on the floor next to the foyer table. Inside it were letters from his grandfather, and in one of those letters his granddad had written his account of the murder and named Con Delancey's killer, or at least his opinion of who had killed him.

Jack couldn't even imagine how the news of the killer's actual identity would affect the Delancey grandchildren. Probably not a lot, he decided. After all, the oldest of them had been only ten when it happened.

Cara Lynn hadn't even been born. He was pretty sure it wouldn't affect her at all. At least Jack hoped it wouldn't. *Whoa*. No, he didn't. He gave his head a mental shake.

Of course he wanted it to affect Cara Lynn. Just as much as the rest of them. He hoped it would gnaw holes in their stomachs that their family had allowed the wrong man to be convicted of murder, just like it gnawed holes in his that his grandfather had been locked up for a quarter of a century for a crime he hadn't committed.

He went inside, grabbed his briefcase from the foyer and set it on the kitchen table, brushing aside a small strip of paper sitting near Cara Lynn's evening bag. He picked it up, thinking to throw it in the trash. It was old, yellowed and brittle, a tiny rounded edge of the flap of an envelope, an old-fashioned *lick-'em, stick-'em* one.

Where had it come from? He stared at it for a few seconds, rubbing one edge between his fingers. It turned to dust. Obviously old. Looking at his dusty fingers, he felt a strong sense that there was something important about it. It had been lying near Cara Lynn's purse. Could that mean it had something to do with the lockbox or its contents?

He stopped and repeated the thought aloud. "The lockbox," he whispered, considering the implications. If it really was an envelope, then that meant there was a letter, didn't it? A letter from whom? Maybe from Cara Lynn's grandmother to her youngest granddaughter, written some time between 1986, when Con Delancey had died, and thirteen years ago when Lilibelle had died. Any paper could have turned yellow and brittle after being stored in a hot place, say an attic, for that long.

But how had Cara Lynn gotten the envelope—or at least that part of it? He looked at her purse, wondering if she'd left the envelope in there. With a furtive glance toward the back of the apartment, he released the clasp on the small rectangular bag and peered inside. No envelope.

So, if she actually had a letter that was inside the box, had she looked at it here at the table? And if she hadn't put it back in her purse, where had she put it?

She had refused to answer his questions about the journal, wanting to know why he was so curious. Of course, he'd been making love to her at the time, and judging by her response to his nips and caresses, she'd been caught up in the pleasure of the moment.

A brief aftershock of lust echoed through him at the memory of how she'd moved beneath him. He immediately shut down those thoughts and made himself think about where she'd have put that envelope. He opened her evening bag and looked inside, feeling a little guilty. He wondered how guilty he'd have felt if he really loved her.

Stepping out of the kitchen and down the hall, he went into the small second bedroom and closed the door. Cara Lynn had made the room into an office. There was a desk and chair, and a drafting table on which a watercolor sketch of a bright wall hanging lay askew. It depicted a nearly abstract cat drawn in black using only three strokes. The hanging would be exquisite as part of her collection at the gallery. He hoped she'd managed to finish putting together the fiber-art version.

He tore his gaze away from the sketch and looked at the bookcases. There, on the third shelf were the gold-etched white leather journals. He took the first one out and opened the cover. On the first page was the hand-written date of June 5, 1951. Lilibelle would have been twelve. There were red sticky flags on some of the pages with tiny scribbled notes in Cara Lynn's neat handwriting. Notes for the genealogy book she was working on for the Delancey and Guillame families.

He quickly scanned the room, but didn't see an envelope. However, it did look as though someone had been in there. The spines of her grandmother's journals were uneven, and there were spaces where books had been removed. Jack picked up the sketch of the black cat and looked beneath it. There was a piece of paper with some notes on it in Cara Lynn's hand. And beneath the paper a journal that should have been on the shelf behind him. He picked it up and put it back. Then he checked around the small room, but he didn't see the envelope.

Back in the kitchen he put the piece of an envelope flap into a plastic baggie. Unlocking his briefcase, he dug under a small stack of architectural drawings and paper-clipped reports down to several rubber-banded stacks of envelopes.

Rifling through them, he found the ones postmarked the earliest. "Okay, Granddad," he whispered. "I met most of the Delanceys tonight. Let's see if my impression of them matches yours."

As he began to read his grandfather's letter for the twentieth time, or the fiftieth, he thought about what he'd told Cara Lynn, about needing to stay up to work on some plans, his implication being that they were architectural drawings.

He smothered a wry laugh. He was working on plans all right—plans to clear his grandfather's name. He'd married Cara Lynn Delancey to gain access to the documents that could help him prove his granddad's innocence. If he broke her heart, well, maybe that would satisfy his need for revenge.

HOURS LATER, JACK rubbed his eyes and yawned. A glance at the kitchen clock told him that his burning eyes and foggy head were telling him the truth. He *had* been up all night. It was after 5:00 a.m.

Cara Lynn would be getting up in about an hour. He should have gone to bed hours ago, but he'd wanted to read over his grandfather's notes while his first impressions of the Delanceys were still fresh in his mind.

He had looked forward to hating every single one of them. But to his surprise, he didn't. They seemed like ordinary people. Okay, maybe not ordinary. He sorted through the letters again until he came to the one where Granddad had listed Con Delancey's grandchildren.

Mr. Delancey's two sons, Michael and Robert, seem rather ordinary, although I can see that they have the genes to be great, like their father. But perhaps Con's philandering and their mother's resentment kept them from achieving everything they could have. In any case, their children—Con's grandchildren—are but babies and it's already obvious they are extraordinary.

Robert, Jr. is the oldest, at nine. Already, it seems to me, he is showing a remarkable resemblance to his grandfather, both in looks and personality. Maybe it's because he's the oldest, but I see in him the most potential of all of them. Mark my word, he'll follow Con into politics, and likely, will be better at it.

Jack took a pencil and jotted a note in the margin, next to the comment. *Died in plane crash at age twenty-three. So much for potential.*

He read the next line. *Lucas, his younger brother, is at age six, already intense, even angry, much like his father. If he continues like this, he'll be a criminal before he's twenty-one. Maybe he can turn himself around.*

Jack remembered Lucas and his wife Angela, who was carrying their first child. Jack wrote in the margin. *Still intense. Channeled into police work.*

Jack continued down the list of Delancey children and his grandfather's impressions of them. A fierce jealousy rose up inside him, as it had every other time he read it. He hated that his grandfather had spent even a few moments thinking about Con Delancey's grandkids and what he saw them becoming as they grew.

But more than that, he hated that his grandfather had been right about them. While he had not been a prophet, he'd certainly been insightful enough to see that Con Delancey's grandkids were extraordinary.

Armand Broussard had thought his own grandson was extraordinary, too. Jack blinked against the sudden stinging in his eyes. He missed his granddad. Had it already been half a year since he'd died? Jack had never seen him in anything except his orange prison jumpsuit, until he looked at him in the casket before the funeral service. That sight, his beloved Papi in a dark suit with that awful makeup and lipstick designed to make the corpse look *natural,* made Jack cry for the first time in his life.

"I'm sorry about that, Papi," he whispered, repeating the same words he'd uttered over his grandfather's body that day at the funeral home. "I couldn't help that. But I swear I will clear your name."

He put the letter back in its ragged envelope, slid the rubber band around the stack and inserted it under the architectural plans and drawings. Then he took out a small spiral bound notebook and paged through it for the notes he'd jotted as he'd read through the letters the first time. After glancing at his handwritten notes, he leaned back in the kitchen chair and stretched.

He didn't have to refer to any notes to recall what his grandfather had said to him at their last meeting. *Ah, Jacques. You are so smart and so wise for your years. But you're drowning your talents in jealousy and hatred. It's no way to live,* mon petit. *It will eat up all the goodness and love inside you and leave you empty and alone. You must forgive them, son. The murder of Con Delancey was only one act by one pathetic individual. The Broussard name is a proud one, but it is not worth the ruination of your life. You can be the better man.*

"I'm sorry, Papi," Jack muttered. "I can never be as good a man as you were."

Standing, Jack locked his briefcase and slipped into the bedroom and lay down beside Cara Lynn, whose back was turned. For a few seconds, he lay and watched her sleep. She was so beautiful, with her eyes closed and her lips slightly parted.

As he'd thought earlier at the reception, she really was one of the most genuine people he'd ever met. Her eyes were always clear and blue, her expression was always open and trusting. He sometimes felt guilty for deceiving her. But it had been the perfect ruse. After all, she was a Delancey, and the Delanceys had ruined his grandfather's life.

As the thoughts flitted drowsily through his mind, his gaze traced the flowing line of her shoulder and torso where the moonlight danced off her skin. He admired the curve of her hips and imagined the shadow centered between them and felt himself harden with desire. He closed his eyes deliberately and turned over, putting his back to hers.

As he did, the bedclothes rustled. After a second, she slid her arm under his and rested her hand on his flat belly. The muscles there contracted when her warm fingers splayed against his skin and the arousal he'd almost managed to quell rose up again.

Desperately, afraid she might decide to slide her hand

lower and coax him into early morning sex, he wrapped her hand in his.

"What time is it?" she asked drowsily.

"Five thirty or so," he said.

"Have you been up all night?"

He nodded. "Told you, I had some plans to go over, but I don't have to go in early today, so I'll have plenty of time to take a nap after you leave."

"Well, in that case…" she murmured in a low voice. At the same time she leaned forward and kissed his bare shoulder.

He grimaced, but he turned onto his back and held up his arm so she could slide into his embrace and rest her head in the little hollow between his neck and shoulder. "I'm way too tired," he said.

She chuckled and the sound of bells filled his ears. "That's disappointing. Maybe next time you'll think twice about staying up all night," she whispered, then nipped at his ear lobe.

The gentle bite startled him and he jumped, which made her laugh harder. He flipped over on top of her hands, then held them in one of his while he tickled her sides.

"Jack, don't!" she cried breathlessly, amid giggling laughter. "I thought you were too—tired."

"Don't what?" he said, slowing down the tickles and allowing them to become caresses. "Don't do this?" he whispered as he slid his hand down her flat belly to caress her. "Or this?" he whispered, pushing into her with a gentle finger.

"Oh—" She wrapped her hand around his wrist, but

not to stop him; she pressed his hand down and arched against it.

Jack felt her readiness and entered her, doing his best to stay disconnected, to keep the coupling casual, but that was never easy with Cara Lynn. She lifted her head to kiss him. As soon as her lips touched his, as soon as he felt her tongue along the seam of his mouth, he reciprocated, cursing himself for being so weak he couldn't resist the person he'd targeted to pay for destroying his grandfather's life.

PAUL GUILLAME LAY awake and watched the purple glow grow lighter in the sky. He felt as though he hadn't slept a wink all night. After seeing Betty Delancey's bestowal of the Guillame fortune on the sweet princess of the Delancey clan, Paul had felt an urge to break one of the expensive bottles of champagne and use its sharp, rough edges to rip all their throats out.

His frustration was that the people whose throats he most wanted to cut were already dead. His Aunt Lilibelle, for one.

She'd yanked him free of the harsh ruling of juvenile court when he was seventeen and raised him as her own, and he'd worshiped her as much as he'd hated her husband, Con. She'd always promised him that he would have her journals. Promised that even after she died, her best friend, Con's sister, Claire, would keep them safe for him.

But years later, when Cara Lynn graduated from high school, she'd been presented with the journals by her mother, who told her that Grandmother Lilibelle had wanted her to have them. Paul protested, but when he saw the first journal, the inscription inside the cover read *To Cara Lynn*, in his beloved Aunt Lili's flowing, decorative hand.

He'd never dreamed that Lili would betray him, not after taking him in to rear along with her own two sons. Not after all the times he'd comforted her when Con was photographed in the company of other women. Not after everything Paul had done for her and everything she'd done for him. They'd always protected each other, and they'd sworn that they always would.

And now, once again he felt the sting of Lili's betrayal. Her last journal, the one that could destroy the Delancey family, had also gone to Cara Lynn along with the Guillame tiara, worth so much it was generally referred to as priceless.

As fascinated as he had always been with the tiara, he wasn't concerned about it. There was an unreal quality about jewels that large. Plus, what good would having the tiara do if he couldn't sell it?

Still, although he was terrified at what someone might find in Lili's last journal, it was some comfort that none of the Delanceys had gotten their hands on it, either. He'd felt a thrill almost as satisfying as a climax when the lights had gone off and people had started shouting and panicking. The seemingly superhuman Delanceys had been as helpless as ordinary people in the face of the sudden, temporary blackout that lasted for only a few minutes until the emergency generator had kicked on.

But the idea that nobody in the room could see, or

know what was happening or who was causing it, had given him a particular thrill. Then when the emergency lights came on and the table was empty—the journal and the tiara gone, he nearly went over the edge.

It had taken every ounce of self-control he had to keep from literally rubbing his palms together with glee. The thief had walked into the Delancey mansion and walked out—or run out—with the journal and the tiara right under the noses of the Delanceys.

But the most exciting thing of all, precisely because he'd been watching Cara Lynn like a hawk all evening, and had made sure his eyes were on *her* and no one else when the lights came on, was that she had covered something with her hand just before the lights went out. Something white and flat, like a sheet of paper or an envelope.

Once the lights were back on, whatever the bit of white had been, it had disappeared as if it had never been there. Three Delancey men were hovering over her, and her husband was standing on a chair, apparently trying to get a good look at the thief.

Paul had kept his eyes on Cara Lynn, but whatever she had found in the journal, she must have secreted it in her purse.

Now, as he picked up the tumbler of bourbon and water he'd left on the nightstand the night before, and drained it, he let his imagination play with what it could be. The most obvious answer was a letter from Lilibelle Guillame to Cara Lynn. But what would Aunt Lili have said to a child who was barely a teenager when she'd died? *Congratulations. Hope you enjoy the nice pres-*

ents? Paul didn't know, but he was damned sure going to find out.

He swallowed the last of the watery bourbon and felt its warmth spread through his insides. The evening had ended better than he could have hoped, for the most part.

He picked up his phone and paged through his contacts until he found the number he was looking for and pressed the Call button. "What the hell happened with your guy?" he asked when the fence, who a buddy of his had put him in touch with, answered.

"Hey, dumbass. Do you know what time it is?" the gruff-voiced man asked.

"To the second. How'd your guy drop the tiara with his fingerprints all over it? Did you have to send the stupidest guy you had?"

The man sighed. "Settle down, will you? You told me yourself there could be five cops there. He was a little nervous."

"Well, he's lucky he dropped the tiara and not the journal."

"How do you figure? That piece was worth a million, easy," the fence said.

"A million, if you count the six recognizable stones that are insured with Lloyd's."

"Yeah. I was just trying to figure out what to do about that. I've got a customer in Japan who might want it just to set it on a shelf—"

"Forget that. We don't have it, remember? Now what about the journal? I haven't heard from your two-bit grab-and-go man."

"Right, right. I know. He was supposed to bring it to me, but he hurt his foot getting out of there."

"So where is it?"

"At his house I guess."

Paul gripped the cell phone so hard his hand cramped. "Well, *get it for me!* Now! That's my journal and I don't want your stupid SOB putting his hands on it. And by the way, when they run the prints from the tiara, you going to try to tell me that he's not going to show up in the system?"

"Yeah. Okay, fine. I'll call him again. I'll get your damn book and bring it to you."

"Don't you dare come near my home. You call me and we'll meet. And then I don't want to ever hear from you again. Got that?"

"Hey. You going to bring me what you owe me?"

Paul laughed. "Maybe half of it, since you haven't even delivered half the goods yet. Call me when you've got the journal."

"No problem, but right now I'm going back to sleep."

Paul hung up.

Shaking his head and thinking he'd have been better off picking up a homeless man to do the job for him, he figured he'd just give up on sleep and get up. He pulled on his sweatpants and sweatshirt and tied his running shoes. At forty-six, he was in good health. He'd been an outstanding long-distance runner in high school, and although he was beginning to feel the effects of his drinking, he'd kept up his routine of running every day, for the most part.

As he jogged along the neutral ground on St. Charles

Street, he decided that it was time—actually past time—for him to make good on his offer to help Cara Lynn with the genealogy she was compiling on the Delancey and Guillame families. That would give him a chance to find the letter she'd hidden in her clutch and keep up with what progress was being made of tracking down the thief.

The papers and documents stored in the attic of Claire Delancey's house would give him an excellent excuse to visit Cara Lynn at her apartment.

His next thought rattled him so much that he lost his jogging rhythm and almost stumbled. Not *her* apartment any longer. *Their* apartment. She'd shocked her entire family by eloping with that yokel, Jack Bush. A fake name if Paul had ever heard one. He couldn't believe the entire Delancey clan had accepted Bush without a peep. But of course, as the baby, Cara Lynn had always been the favorite. Her brothers and cousins probably thought when she spoke that flowers and fairies spilled from her mouth.

Paul slowed his pace. Suddenly his heart was racing and his breath was short. He needed to stop his habit of keeping a glass on his nightstand. It was possible that a couple of fingers of bourbon first thing in the morning was bad for his stamina. He made a mental note to stop doing that.

Meanwhile, he needed to go digging in that box in the attic for birth records, marriage licenses and photos so he could make a fabulous first impression on Cara Lynn. Then, once he'd established himself as a regular visitor, he could search for the letter. He had to get his hands on it. He'd never have expected Claire to die so suddenly. She had never seemed old. Even in her seventies, she'd seemed enduring, immortal.

Now, he was desperate to get his hands on every bit of information Lili had given her about that dreadful day. Con's death had haunted him for almost thirty years, and he knew he would never be at ease until he was certain there was *nothing* in writing from Lilibelle that could reveal what really happened.

He'd never harbored a lot of love for the baby of the Delancey family, Cara Lynn. But he didn't want to hurt her if he didn't have to. For that matter, he didn't want to hurt anyone. But he would if he had to, to protect himself.

Chapter Four

On Sunday morning, Jack slept late. He was just getting up when Cara Lynn came in to tell him she was on her way to her studio. "It'll probably be after dark when I get back," she said. "I've got one piece that's not finished and another that I need to stretch and hang. If I don't get them done, I'll have two gigantic empty spaces on the wall when the show opens tomorrow night."

"Sit down here," he murmured sleepily, pushing himself up against the headboard and reaching for her hand.

"Jack, I don't have time," she said with a smile.

"Were you able to finish the cat?"

"The cat?" Her eyes widened. She hadn't told him about the mixed-media wall hanging because it wasn't finished yet. "How do you know about the cat?"

"I saw your sketch in the office. I like it a lot."

"Really? You do?" Cara Lynn wasn't sure why she'd started that piece. Most of her fiber-art pieces were more abstract. But she'd sketched out the long, sleek body of the cat in her mind one night after she and Jack had made love. To her, the cat was a representation of

Jack. The beauty of his body, his careless, unconscious grace and, most of all, the regal, arrogant tilt to his head.

"Sure. There's something about it. I like the strong lines."

Just as he finished speaking, his cell phone rang. She glanced toward where it lay on the bedside table, but he grabbed it and looked at the display kind of furtively, she thought. But once he saw who it was, he relaxed and answered it. "Sure, Ryker. We can do that."

Her cousin Ryker was a detective for the St. Tammany Parish Sheriff's Office, which served Chef Voleur. If he was calling Jack, maybe that meant they'd found the thief.

"What about the journal, and—I see. Sure. Hang on." He looked up. "We need to go by the sheriff's office. They want us to sign our statements and take a look at some mug shots to see if we can identify the thief. When can you go?"

"Now," she said. "Before I go to the studio."

Jack told Ryker that and said that he'd be there a little later, then hung up.

"Did they find the journal?" she asked eagerly.

"He didn't say anything about having recovered the journal, but he did say they're following up on a lead on a suspect. They apparently got fingerprints off the tiara."

"That's good. I hope they have the journal. I can't wait to see it." She looked at her watch and blew out a frustrated breath. "I've got to hurry, though, because once I finish with the pieces, I should take them on down to the gallery."

He patted the bed beside him. "Sit down here for a minute. I want to look at your head."

She sat and leaned forward until her forehead was less than an inch from his eye. "See?"

He chuckled. "I see what looks like a strip bandage, but it's too blurry to tell for sure." He pushed up to a seated position in the bed. "Now."

She sat beside him and he quickly peeled the bandage off and checked the cut on her forehead.

"It looks good. How does your shoulder feel?"

She flexed it and winced. "It's fine."

"Take something," he admonished her. "Some ibuprofen or something. Don't just suffer."

She kissed him quickly, managing to land the kiss before he could move to get up and avoid it. One of these days she was going to have to ask him why he didn't want to kiss her. Because she was sure it wasn't just missed timing. She'd seen him recoil the night before. And even if she weren't sure about the other times—which she was—she was definitely sure of that one. He'd deliberately dodged her.

Jack slipped out of bed and headed to the bathroom.

She watched him, thinking how much she loved looking at his perfect body and how much she loved being held and kissed and loved by him.

No. Maybe she shouldn't ask him why he didn't want to kiss her. She might be crushed by his answer.

Jack stepped into the bathroom, which was still steamy and fragrant from Cara Lynn's shower. As he opened the shower door and turned on the hot water, she came up behind him and slid her arms around his waist and pressed a kiss to his shoulder. "Mmm, you smell warm, like my husband. Are you going with me?"

Jack frowned. "To the sheriff's office? No. You heard me tell Ryker I'd be there a little later."

"No," she said, moving her lips against his shoulder. "To the gallery."

"What for? I'm going to be busy all day. Those plans I'm working on are a tricky design and it's probably going to take me several more hours to finish it."

She nuzzled his shoulder, then moved up and kissed the nape of his neck. "Not today. Tomorrow night. For the opening. There will be hors d'oeuvres and wine. It's semi-formal."

He stepped away from her kiss. "Sure. Give me the name of the gallery and the time and I'll meet you there."

"I want you to go *with* me."

"Depends on what time you're leaving. You're probably wanting to get there early, but the reason I've got to finish that design today is because I've got a meeting in Biloxi tomorrow afternoon. I might be cutting it really close."

She gave him an odd, almost hurt look. "Okay. I'll go by myself and you can come when you get back. Mom said she'd be there, and I guarantee you she'll invite us over for coffee afterward. She already tried to get me to come over for dinner before the show."

"Why don't you go? She just wants to have you around."

"I can't eat before a show, and besides, I'll probably still be working on the finishing touches for the two pieces."

"Okay, then," he said, and moved to kiss her on the cheek, but she intercepted him with her mouth and gave him a kiss that promised everything he'd ever wanted and more. He responded with a sense of surrender. He was going to be in big trouble if he had no more defenses against her than to get caught by such a simple ploy. He should have anticipated her last-second feint. Sometimes he was afraid she was much smarter than he was. Very afraid. If she was as smart as he was beginning to think she was, he probably didn't have a chance of fooling her for very long. He needed to get the proof that would exonerate his grandfather and get the heck out of there before she started putting things together. All these thoughts zipped through his mind the one-tenth of a second between her stopping the kiss and speaking. Because while she was kissing him he hadn't been able to think anything except *More, more, more.*

"Bye, handsome," she said, flicking him on the nose.

"So long, beautiful," he responded, not looking at her. He listened to her heels click on the hardwood as she walked up the hall. He heard her stop in the office, then turn around and come back to the bedroom.

"By the way, when you were in my office, did you take down one of my grandmother's journals?" she asked him.

"No, why?"

She sat down on the bed. "One of Grandmother's journals is on the table instead of on the shelf. And it's under my sketch of the cat."

"I saw it. I figured you'd left it there."

"No." She stared at him for a few seconds. "So if you didn't leave it there, then I'm worried that someone really is coming in when we're not here."

"*If* I didn't?" Jack repeated. "What the hell, Cara Lynn? Don't you believe me?"

She seemed taken aback. "No, of course I believe you. Didn't you mention it earlier? About that bottle of water being missing?" She glanced up briefly, then turned her head to look toward the office. "But, you're sure you didn't forget—while you were looking at the sketch maybe?"

"I didn't move your stuff," he snapped, a lot more irritated by her implication than he should have been.

"Okay," she said, irritation sharpening her voice as well. She stood and left the bedroom again. As she walked out, he heard her mutter, "I *know* it wasn't me," then heard the front door open and close.

He'd thought he would need a cool shower after that kiss. But now he decided he'd better stick with hot and steamy so it would dissolve his anger at Cara Lynn. He was guilty of enough already. He didn't need her suspicious of him for things he hadn't even done.

He showered quickly, dressed in jeans and a T-shirt and felt a hundred percent better. In the living room, he opened the blinds and checked the parking lot to be sure Cara Lynn's car was gone. Then he headed for the kitchen, thinking about her certainty that one of her grandmother's journals had been moved, and a little worried that *if* someone were coming into the apartment, they might have tried to open his briefcase.

With a sudden sense of apprehension, Jack checked its latch. It was locked. He breathed a sigh of relief. He realized with a sinking feeling that after staying up all night, he couldn't have sworn in a court of law that he'd locked it.

He glanced around the kitchen as he thought about the night before. When he'd come in, Cara Lynn had been hurrying out of the pantry with an armful of water bottles that weren't needed in the refrigerator. The fact that a bottle was missing seemed to surprise her as much as it surprised him. So why had she brought three more from the pantry? She'd looked a little frazzled and a little guilty, as if he'd interrupted something.

He stopped and closed his eyes, trying to remember just exactly what had happened right before the lights went out. Unfortunately, he hadn't been looking in her direction when the room went dark. He'd been talking to Paul Guillame. So no, he hadn't seen a thing.

However, Paul had been looking that way. Then when the lights came back on and the journal and the tiara were missing, Jack had immediately jumped up onto the chair to see if he could spot the thief running away. It had only been when he'd heard Cara Lynn calling for him that he'd turned to her.

Damn it. If he'd been more careful about staying in his role as loving husband, he might have seen her hide the letter.

He understood that he was basing the existence of a letter on a tiny scrap of brittle paper and he knew that could be sheer folly. For all he knew, the scrap might have nothing to do with the journal. Cara Lynn could have been paging through ancient recipe books and come across one written on the back of an envelope. She loved reading her grandmother and mother's handwritten recipes. Or it could easily be an old document she'd acquired for her genealogy. Actually, that was the most likely source, but for some reason, Jack couldn't let go of the idea that the scrap had come from the same box that had held the journal and tiara.

It seemed natural that Cara Lynn's grandmother would have written her a note about the items she was leaving her. Even if it was nothing more than *Best wishes. I love you.*

But if that's what it was, then why hide it? What could be so secretive about a letter from a grandmother to her youngest granddaughter? Was Cara Lynn just a naturally suspicious person? The kind of person who would hide anything until she'd had a chance to read it? No. Cara was definitely *not* that kind of person. He'd known her intimately for two months. Granted that wasn't long, but his impression was that she was as honest and open as the day was long. She seemed to him like the last person on the planet who would just decide to hide something on a whim. He didn't think she'd had time to glance at it, not without a lot of people noticing and asking about it.

Maybe where her family was concerned, she *was* secretive. If he were in a family filled with cops and lawyers and special forces operatives, he'd be damned careful about what he did and did not share with them.

His first thought was that the letter had something to do with Con Delancey's murder. But that was *his* obses-

sion. Even if the letter was from Lilibelle Guillame and
stated outright that Armand Broussard was not the murderer, there would be no reason for Cara Lynn to hide it
or keep the information a secret from him or from her
family. It would have been a topic of lively conversation and possibly heated arguments, at least for a short
while until something else caught their imagination.

But he could not think of another thing that could
be in the letter. Unless it was just a *Dear Cara Lynn, I
wanted you to have this*...note. Or possibly a letter Lili
had written to her best friend Claire. *Claire, please
keep these safe for me. One day, perhaps when she
marries, I'd love for the journals and the tiara to go
to the youngest, Cara Lynn. She reminds me so much
of myself when I was that age. Maybe she'll read my
journals and decide she wants to write. Maybe she'll
use the tiara to give herself a nest egg, so she won't be
trapped in a loveless marriage....*

Jack stopped his thoughts. He was drifting off into
daydreams—or daymares. Why in the world would he
think that Cara Lynn's grandmother had feared—or
prophesized—that her youngest granddaughter might
be trapped in a marriage without love? That was just
his own guilt coming out.

Having interrupted his train of thought, Jack forced
himself to continue thinking rationally instead of fan-
tasizing. He had no business trying to find the letter.
There was probably less than a one percent chance that
it had anything at all to do with his grandfather.

He sat down at the kitchen table and unlocked his

briefcase. He wanted to review the police report from the first officer on the scene after Con Delancey was shot.

He'd hired a private investigator a few weeks ago, hoping to get his hands on any unreleased police records regarding Armand Broussard. Jack was certain that there were forms or reports he hadn't thought or known to ask for. It had been over a week since he'd talked to the P.I. and he was anxious to hear from him.

He dug through the letters and found the stack he was looking for. As he pulled the letters out, his eye was caught by the baggie that held the yellowed scrap of envelope. He studied it for a moment, then glanced toward the pantry door. Cara Lynn had acted downright guilty when she'd come out of the pantry with the bottles in her hands.

She had hidden the letter somewhere in there. Suddenly, it didn't matter to him that there was a 99 percent chance that the letter was of no interest to him—or to anyone except Cara Lynn. There was always that 1 percent. What if there was something—even if it was one sentence or one phrase—that might give him a clue to help clear his grandfather's name?

He glanced at his watch. He needed to get to the police station and sign his statement, but right now he was alone in the house and was going to be alone all day. He might not have a better chance to search for the letter for a long time.

He went into the pantry and eyed the shelves filled with cans, canisters, boxes and bags of food. Everything from staples like flour and sugar and cornmeal to gourmet items like escargot, Major Grey's chutney, fancy crackers and aged balsamic vinegar. He glanced through the shelves, thinking if she'd been clever enough to hide a thin envelope amongst all the food, it would take him a lot longer than an hour or so to find it.

So figuring it would be faster to eliminate obvious hiding places first, he started investigating the room. A loose floor board or baseboard or a cubby hole cut into the wall would make a great hiding place. At that instant, his toe hit something that rattled loosely. He bent down and looked underneath the bottom shelf. He had to move a case of bottled water from which three were missing, but when he did, he hit pay dirt. A piece of baseboard toppled over.

He bent down and looked at the hole. He could see the corner of a yellowed envelope. His pulse raced. *There it was.* Whether it might be of any help to him, he had no idea. But at least he'd know.

He slid the envelope out carefully and looked at it. On the front were the words *for Cara Lynn,* written in a beautiful, old-fashioned script. He turned the envelope over. The flap was held in place with two inches of brown, dried-out cellophane tape across the center. The right edge of the flap had been torn off. That was the piece he'd found. This was definitely the same envelope.

But then he saw that there was a newer piece of tape that ran across part of the older tape. Someone had opened the envelope and closed it back. The tape wasn't brand new—so it hadn't happened recently.

He tried to lift the edge of the new tape with a fingernail, but it pulled a crumbling piece of the envelope's flap with it.

"Damn it," he muttered, as he carefully pressed the tape down again. He couldn't get into it without destroying it and the tape that held it so precariously. He looked at the front again. The decorative handwriting had been penned with a fountain pen. There was a tiny bit of ink spatter underneath the *C* in *Cara Lynn*. Also, the pen had left thick lines in some places and needle-thin lines in others.

That settled it. He couldn't open the envelope without destroying it and he'd never be able to replace it. Sighing, he sank to his haunches again and started to replace the board. But his curiosity got the better of him. He reached into the hole again.

The first thing his fingers touched was a roll of bills. He pulled them out and tried to estimate how much money was there. Maybe a couple of thousand, he thought. He reached in a third time and pulled out her passport. He flipped through it, stopping at the front to check the expiration date. The passport was good for ten more months.

He stared at the date, thinking that their marriage would certainly expire before the passport would. How would she take it, he wondered, then immediately cleared his throat loudly and forced his brain to cut off that line of thought.

The third thing he found in the hole concealed by the baseboard was a velvet jewelry case—a necklace case, by the shape of it. He opened it and immediately realized he was looking at probably twenty, thirty, even forty thousand dollars' worth of real, mined emeralds. The necklace was exquisite, with small diamonds on either side of each larger emerald, and a two-inch long teardrop emerald pendant hanging from the center of the piece. He closed the case and stuck it back.

He'd known when he started this venture that he and his family were paupers compared to the Delanceys, but looking at those ridiculously huge gemstones slammed his face into just how different they were. As he carefully replaced everything including the envelope, then put the baseboard back and rearranged the water bottles, he thought it was a good thing that he wasn't serious about Cara Lynn.

Because as soon as their honeymoon was over, the feelings of her family would begin to weigh on her mind, and eventually, they'd convince her that she'd made a big mistake. That she'd married way beneath her.

As for him, he had sense enough to know he was so far out of her league he wasn't even in her zip code. Yep, it was a good thing he was only in this for revenge and not for love.

He glanced at his watch. He was going to have to wait to go over his granddad's letter. He had to get to the sheriff's office. As he stood and started to lock the case, his cell phone rang. He looked at the display.

It was Greg Haymore, the private investigator he'd hired for an outrageous sum that he hoped would be totally worth it. Haymore was a good investigator, but his real value was in his connections.

Haymore was a former police officer who'd been fired for suborning perjury in a court case involving the shooting death of his partner. He'd lied about whether his partner had a throwaway gun, afraid that if the jury knew that the officer was carrying a secret weapon, they'd assume the officer was crooked and let the killer off. Haymore's good intentions got the killer acquitted and himself fired.

"Hey, Jack, what's going on?" Haymore said when Jack answered the phone.

"Nothing much. What's up?"

"You enjoying married life?"

Jack winced. He'd had to tell Haymore some of his plan, and their contract included a severe non-disclosure agreement, but damn it, he didn't have to listen to the man's ribbing. "Did you have something for me?"

"Yeah." The investigator's voice took on a professional tone. "I've got a buddy on the Chef Voleur Police Force that's—"

"Whoa. You can't go messing with them. I told you, a bunch of the Delanceys are police officers or detectives—at least two of them, twins, are in Chef Voleur—and they're not stupid, not by a long shot. If you screw this up, man, there is nowhere in the world that you'll be able to get another job."

"Listen, I know what I'm doing, and this guy is a sergeant. He's a good guy and he never liked Con Delancey. He knows the two officers—as he calls them, the Delancey Bobbsey Twins—and there's no love lost there, either. He was happy to take a look at this case's evidence file for me."

"The evidence file?" Jack was interested in spite of his concern over Haymore taking unnecessary chances.

"Yeah. He said there are unused samples of blood

in there. Said if you could get an order for DNA, you might find out something that would help exonerate your grandfather."

"Blood," Jack repeated thoughtfully. He thought about the implications of having blood samples from twenty-eight years ago. That was before DNA sampling was widely understood or affordable for anyone but the government. Today was a completely different story. DNA could be used to identify someone to a one in many, many billions of accuracy.

"Okay. That could be promising. But Greg, I want you to sit on that for now. And please—I just hope your source is as trustworthy as you think he is."

"Oh, he's good. His name is—"

"No. I don't want to know his name. Just make sure that nobody, and I mean *nobody* else knows about this. I'll let you know if and when I want to use it. Okay?"

"This might be exactly what you're looking for, Jack. A DNA match might deliver the real killer right into your hands."

"I know. I'm just not sure how to go about it. You sit tight. I don't want you doing anything else right now. Got that? I'll let you know when I need you again. I'll deposit your fees up to now into your account. And Greg? Thanks."

"No problem," Haymore said. "I'll be watching for that deposit. Talk to you later."

"Oh, hang on a second," Jack said. "One more question. Did you hear about the robbery at the Delancey residence Saturday night?"

"Yeah. Not much on the news, but there's talk everywhere about it. Somebody just walked in and stole that Guillame tiara?"

"He dropped the tiara—not on purpose I'm sure. But he did take a journal written by Lilibelle Guillame. Do you know anything about the thief? Or know anybody who does things like that? That bold I mean?"

"Walk in, grab a million-dollar piece of jewelry and then run out, right through a crowd of rich folks and cops? Nah."

"If you hear anything, give me a call on my cell, okay?"

"Sure thing, Bush."

After Jack hung up, he sat there, thinking about the idea of using DNA to prove who killed Con Delancey. DNA was proof-positive. One hundred percent. No more doubt. No more questions.

For the first time in his life, Jack actually wondered if he was doing the right thing. For the first time in his life, he considered the possibility that his grandfather had killed Con Delancey.

Chapter Five

Cara Lynn smiled at the elderly couple who were walking hand-in-hand around the gallery, admiring the paintings, sculptures and other art pieces.

She was waiting for Jack and about to scream. Her mother had just arrived and was talking to the gallery owner. Cara Lynn was doing what she was supposed to do, making herself available to the patrons and guests. But she thought if she had to stand there smiling and answering questions and listening to comments and critiques one more minute, she might have a psychotic break, right in the middle of one of the most prestigious galleries in the Warehouse District of New Orleans.

She'd had all day to consider what she was going to do about what she'd found under the kitchen table, but she was no closer to an answer than she'd been that morning when she'd discovered the small, spiral-bound notepad.

Since seeing it on the floor against one of the table legs and picking it up, she'd opened it at least a dozen times to flip through for one more look at the notes he'd made about his grandfather, about her grandfather, about her family—about *her*.

Reading Jack's notes had been painful, the way a sore tooth was. The kind of pain that kept the tongue coming back to test it, as if by repeatedly touching it, the pain would—what? Give up and stop hurting?

But Jack's notebook hadn't given up. Nor had it stopped hurting her. No matter where she turned, no matter whose name she saw, whether it was hers or someone in her family or his, it hurt just as much. And yet she kept probing.

She'd stopped time and time again all day long to look through the little spiral-bound book, after that first time, when she'd flopped down on the floor and read it cover to cover without stopping except to dry her tears. After that, she'd looked for something—a paragraph, a sentence, even a word or two, that Jack had written that told her he cared about her. So far, she hadn't turned up anything.

Jack's sketchy notes were the antithesis of her grandmother Lilibelle's poetic, flowing narrative. But both of them, in their way, were documenting history as it occurred.

Jack had documented the history of how he'd pursued her, arranged to bump into her, and finally met and seduced her into falling for him.

As she'd paged through the notebook for the first time, she'd come to a page where he'd written her name and age, the words *fiber artist,* and a list of her gallery showings and sales. He'd listed an interview she'd done a few weeks before and jotted a note about her working on a genealogy of the Delancey and Guillame families.

On the next page he'd written the showing at the Donnelly Gallery a second time, along with its date, plus four scribbled words. *Accidentally bump into her.*

She shivered, standing there in the art gallery just like she had the first time she'd read those words. On the following page were more scribbled notations.

7/14—Spent the nite—her apt. Nice! Sexy!
Likes pasta—a lot. Talks about family.
Shouldn't be hard.

Biting her lip and feeling her cheeks turn hot with embarrassment at some of the things Jack had alluded to, she turned the pages until she got to the first thing that had caught her eye that morning. It was the name Con Delancey.

It was over halfway through the pad, behind Jack's notes. Dog-eared pages that held tiny sketches and dimensions and calculations, all of which she assumed had to do with Jack's architecture business. She remembered flipping through, a small smile on her face as she looked at what she thought were her husband's work notes. A small thrill had hummed through her at the anticipation of seeing her name in there, maybe with a note about what time to meet her for the fiber-art show opening, or a note to himself to pick up flowers or something for her.

But when she'd seen her grandfather's name, she'd stopped and read the entire page, and a knot of fear had lodged under her breastbone. That page and several others had been filled with notes that referred to

Con's death, Lilibelle's obsession with journaling, and the address of the fishing cabin on Lake Pontchartrain.

She flipped through the entire notebook, each page a hopeful encounter that gave her one more chance to find out that she was wrong. That the notes and dates and comments would coalesce into something innocuous. But when she turned a page and saw the name Armand Broussard, and below it the charges against him, then below that, *INNOCENT!!!* in block letters, she knew there were no innocuous explanations.

Then, when she saw the very last page, there was no denying the truth. It was plain to see. And it hurt. The last page was where Jack had experimented with new names until he'd decided on Jack Bush.

Jacques Broussard.

Jack Broussard. Jack Bruce. Jack Bushman.

Jack Bush. *Jack Bush.*

Cara Lynn still felt the chill that had flash-frozen her heart. She'd dropped the notebook and covered her mouth with her hands, doing her best to hold in a shocked scream. Her husband was Armand Broussard's grandson.

Jacques Broussard. Her husband Jack was Jacques Broussard. His grandfather had killed hers. Jack had found her, studied her, seduced her into a whirlwind marriage so he could—*what?* What exactly did he want so badly that had required making her fall in love with him and marry him?

BY THE TIME Jack got back from Biloxi that evening and made it to the gallery, it was late and the guests were thinning out. The only hors d'oeuvres left were little pigs in blankets and the only drinks were a mint-julep punch and a chardonnay which had grown warm. He bypassed the food and drink and headed toward Cara Lynn, who did not look happy. He wondered if the showing had gone really badly, or maybe she was getting a migraine. Deep inside, though, a queasy dread told him he knew what the real problem was.

He stepped up to her and touched the small of her back. She jumped slightly but didn't acknowledge his presence in any other way.

"Sorry I was late," he whispered. "I didn't realize they were going to take the meeting through dinner. But the good news is, I think I'm going to get a huge contract to design their new casino."

Cara Lynn smiled and nodded to the couple who wandered away while Jack was speaking. She didn't acknowledge him.

"Cara, hon, are you all right? How did the show go?"

She nodded distractedly. "Fine," she said tightly. "I sold three pieces. What more could I ask?"

Jack studied her. Her mouth was compressed, her shoulders were rigid. He could feel the tension running through the muscles of her back. She was seriously upset. He slid his hand around her waist and pulled her closer, but she neatly extracted herself from his grasp as her mother approached.

"What a wonderful show, Cara Lynn! You and Jack are coming by the house for coffee, aren't you?"

"No, Mom," Cara Lynn said tiredly. "I'm exhausted and I'm sure Jack is, too. He just managed to get here from Biloxi, I believe." With that, she shot Jack a look that should have fried him on the spot.

"Come on," he said. "Let's get home." He gave Cara Lynn's mother a nod. "I apologize, Mrs. Delancey. We'll see you another night. I'll look forward to it."

He led Cara Lynn out and asked her if she would be okay driving her car home. "If not, I'll drive us and I can get someone to bring the car out tomorrow."

"I'm fine," Cara Lynn said archly. "Believe me, I am not drunk."

"I didn't say you were. You just told your mother you were too exhausted to spend half an hour with her."

"So?"

Jack sent her a questioning look, but she just turned on her heel and walked to her car. He watched until she pulled out of the parking lot, then he got into his car and followed her to their apartment.

All the way home, he tried to convince himself that there were all kinds of reasons for her behavior. It wasn't necessarily because she'd found his notepad and read it. She could have a headache and be truly exhausted. She could be coming down with something. She could have gotten angry at him for a dozen reasons that might not make any sense to him. But he wasn't fooling himself. There was only one reason she'd look at him like that. Only one reason she'd be so pale and rigid.

When he got inside, she was standing at the kitchen table, her arms folded, as if she were holding on to herself as tightly as she could. Her face was pale and wan except for two spots of color that stood out in her cheeks. If her glare were a laser, he'd be cut in two.

"Okay, what's wrong?" he asked as his hands became clammy and his pulse sped up until blood hammered in his ears.

He'd gotten to the meeting in Biloxi to discuss a contract for a new casino and realized he didn't have his notepad where he kept his ideas and reminders. It wasn't in his briefcase. It wasn't in his car and it wasn't in his pocket. He'd managed to get through the meeting without too many problems, but from the instant he realized the notebook was gone, a lump of apprehension had lodged in his throat.

Standing there in front of Cara Lynn, the apprehension turned to certainty. He knew exactly what was wrong with Cara Lynn and exactly what was about to happen.

The jig was up.

Struggling to put a tone of casual weariness in his voice, he said, "I hope it's something simple, because it has been a long day and I'm exhausted."

"I'm sure you are. It must be hard, maintaining a cover story 24/7. Of course it's probably a lot simpler if you can spend a large percentage of that time having sex. That saves time having to pretend, I guess."

"What?" Jack said, frowning. He heard her words, but he couldn't quite make sense of them. But certain things began becoming clear, like *cover story*, *pretend*, *sex*. "Cara Lynn, I'm not sure what you're—"

"Save it," she snapped. "How long did you think you could last before you let something slip? Said something suspicious? Or—" She held up his notepad. "Or left something lying around?"

"Cara Lynn—hold on a minute."

"No. I don't need to hold on. I shouldn't have even let you come back here, but I felt like I deserved at least a little bit of an explanation. I feel humiliated, violated and of course stupid...." She paused to take a deep breath and swipe at her eyes with her fingers.

Jack wished there was a way he could comfort her and convince her that he hadn't used her. He wished they lived in a world where he could snap his fingers and everything that both of them knew about their grandfathers would disappear and it would be only the two of them. He wished he hadn't humiliated, violated and betrayed her. But this was reality.

He'd made this bed of snakes, and now he was going to have to sleep in it. He spread his palms—knowing that by doing so he was acknowledging and agreeing to everything she'd said.

"You're not even going to try and deny it?" she asked, but even if he'd wanted to or been able to answer, she was still too quick. She continued before he managed to recall how to breathe, much less speak.

"Tell me, Jacques, did you get what you wanted? And was it worth prostituting yourself?"

Cara Lynn forced those last words out past a growing lump in her throat. The lump felt as big as a levee and it blocked the tears that wanted to break free and fall. If it would just last a few more minutes, until she'd finished what she wanted to say, then she could throw Jacques Broussard out of her home and out of her life, and she'd be free to cry all she wanted to.

"That's what you did, you know," she added. "You

prostituted yourself. But I guess that's not as difficult for men as it is for women."

She steeled herself and met his gaze. He looked shell-shocked, and his mouth was open as if he wanted to say something, but couldn't quite get it out. She'd have liked to gloat over his misery, but she was too busy right now, trying to keep the tears at bay. "What?" she snapped. "What is it?"

He shook his head. "Cara Lynn, I never meant to hurt you. You have to understand. As much as you loved your grandparents, I loved mine, too. And my grandfather didn't kill yours."

"First of all I don't *have* to do anything—" Cara Lynn stopped talking as soon as Jack's last words penetrated. "Oh, no," she said. "You will not just walk in here after what you've done and say *Armand Broussard didn't kill Con Delancey*. Of course he did. He was arrested and convicted and put in prison."

"That doesn't mean he was guilty," Jack said. "It just shows how much influence the Delancey family had. And please, you don't need to tell me what happened to *my* grandfather. Yes, he was arrested and convicted of Con Delancey's murder. He was sent to prison in 1987, and he stayed there until six months ago. Do you know what happened six months ago?" he asked.

She didn't say anything, waiting for him to go on.

"Well?" he snapped. "Do you?"

She shook her head.

"Of course you don't, because neither you nor your entire family have ever bothered to learn anything about Armand Broussard. He served as your grandfather's personal assistant for over twenty years. He handled his correspondence, both personal and official, he acted as his valet, and he was his best friend." Jack hardly paused to take a breath.

"My grandfather loved and respected Con Delancey and Con loved and respected him. He left him a quarter of a million dollars in his will, but of course the Delanceys couldn't let the man they'd decided was guilty of his murder inherit any of his money."

Cara Lynn stared at the man she'd fallen in love with and married within one month of meeting him. He was angry—really angry, for the first time ever. He looked different. His eyes were dark and glittering. His face was masked with rage. The tendons in his neck and wrists stood out in sharp outline against his skin.

"But my grandfather never cared about the money. All he ever wanted to do was clear his name. A name you probably barely recognized—if you even did at all. To you, he's just a nonentity out there. He killed a relative of yours that you've never met for a reason you've probably never even been curious about in a time before you were born. You have no connection to your grandfather, my grandfather or the incident that changed my grandfather's life and his family's lives forever. You have no clue what our life was like because someone in your family decided to kill Con Delancey and frame my granddad for the murder." He pounded his chest twice with his fist.

Cara Lynn had nothing to say. In a rather hazy, stunned way, she realized that what he'd said was true. She had no sense of connection to Con Delancey. He was her grandfather, but she knew nothing about him except that he was murdered.

"Well?" he said again. "I asked you a question. Do you know why my grandfather is no longer in prison as of six months ago? Not because he was paroled. Not because his sentence was up." Jack shook his head and pressed his lips together. "My grandfather is no longer in prison because he died. He *died* in prison. And do you know what he said with his last breath? He said he loved me and he hoped I believed he was innocent."

Cara Lynn heard the emotion in his voice. The rage in his face had morphed into grief and sadness, and dampness gleamed in his eyes. She understood that he was loyal to his grandfather. That he wanted his grandfather to be innocent.

She understood, because she wanted the same thing—for him. But not at the expense of breaking the hearts of her family. She longed to reach out to Jack, even after what he'd done to her. But she steeled herself against him. "But if your grandfather didn't kill my grandfather, then who did?" she asked.

Jack leveled a gaze at her. "There aren't many choices for the answer to that question."

"What are you saying?"

"I'm saying there were only three people at the fishing cabin that weekend."

"How do you know that?"

"Because Papi told me."

"Papi?"

"My grandfather."

Cara Lynn felt a pang deep inside her. "You call him

Papi?" she asked. The idea that he had a nickname for his grandfather sliced her heart in two.

"You're right," she said, her voice small. "I don't have a connection with my grandfather. He hasn't meant as much to me as your Papi has to you. To me, he's a story—a legend. I never had a chance to know him, to talk with him." She paused for a second. "To give him a nickname like Papi or Grampa or—" She shrugged. "He'd died before I was born. He was a great man with a great future, so I *hear*. But his life was snuffed out way before his time—because of *your* grandfather, Armand Broussard."

"*Not* because of my grandfather!" Jack shouted.

Suddenly, his anger ignited hers. It piled in on top of all of her other emotions. It was heavy, overpowering and it tamped down on the hurt and heartbreak that still swirled inside her at Jack's betrayal.

"Stop it!" she cried. "I'm not going to stand here and listen to this. It's not true. Any of it. You're deluded if you think you can clear your grandfather's name. You can't clear the name of a person who's guilty. I need you to get out of here, now! I don't want to ever lay eyes on you again. Can you understand that? Never!" To her horror and dismay, the tears got past the lump and started to fall from her eyes. "Oh, damn it," she sobbed.

"Oh, hell no, I'm not leaving. You can forget that. Remember what we talked about the other morning. Someone has been coming in here when we're gone. And that means that you could be in danger. There is no way I'm leaving you here by yourself."

"I don't need you. I'll call my brothers. They'll take

care of me. In fact—I'll call Lucas. He'll find some-thing to arrest you for. Or Travis. He's a former army special forces officer. He could make you disappear without a trace. Harte can prosecute you for—for—" She stopped because Jack was grinning. Not the false smile he'd given her so often, but a real grin. And that made her so angry that she thought smoke might be coming out of her ears. "Stop laughing at me! What?"

"There's no way you're getting your brothers or your cousins or anyone else in your family involved."

She stared at him. "Are you threatening me?"

He shook his head.

"Then what? Making fun? Never mind." She cut a hand through the air. "I don't care what you're doing. You just sit back and watch me. All I have to do is make one phone call and all four of my brothers will be over here so fast you'll think they flew."

Jack tried to wipe the grin off his face. She could tell he was trying. But she could still see the shadow of amusement in his eyes.

"Oh, I don't doubt that," he said. "But how many times have you told me how they tease you and make fun of you and check up on your dates? How they act like you can't do anything without their help. What do you think they're going to do when they find out that you were duped by the grandson of Armand Brous-sard?"

"You *wish* my brothers would make fun of me," she said. "They're going to be all over you. They're going to feel so sorry for me, because of what…you…did…." her words trailed off as she listened to what she was saying. *Damn it.* He was right. She'd almost rather die than have to tell them that Jack married her to get revenge on the Delancey family. In fact, she'd almost rather die than tell them who Jack really was.

They *would* be all over him. They might hurt him. But even worse than what they would do to Jack, was what they would do to her. It would all be for her own good and because they loved her and because they wanted to protect her of course. She could hear it all now. But the unbearable truth was that they would feel sorry for her, and that meant they would treat her with even more delicacy than they already did—because of course poor little Cara Lynn would have a broken heart. And at the same time, they'd make fun of her until she'd be tempted to torture and kill each one of them—as slowly and painfully as possible.

They'd do everything they possibly could to make everything right again. Of course they would never succeed, not this time. But by God they'd kill themselves and smother her trying.

Damn him. Jack was absolutely right. There was no way she could bring any of her family into this. Not unless she became desperate. And she meant *really desperate.*

But what about Jack? He had already declared that he wouldn't leave her alone and vulnerable. But could she believe him? She had no idea. Still, her only choice was to stay right by Jack's side and make sure he couldn't prove that Armand Broussard was innocent. Because if Broussard was innocent, that meant that her grandfather was killed by someone in her own family. And that couldn't be true. Could it?

JACK SLEPT ON the couch that night. Or, more truthfully, he lay on the couch, wide awake, and listened to Cara Lynn's quiet crying in the bedroom. A loud click told him she'd latched the bedroom door. That stopped his notion that he might try to comfort her.

Comfort her? Him? Who was he trying to kid? If he went in there, she'd probably throw a lamp at him. He was the reason she was crying. She wouldn't take comfort from him if he were the last man on earth. Her muffled sobs echoed around him, making him feel lower than whale droppings.

His grandfather had admonished him to be the *better man*. Well, he wasn't. He never would be. He'd done this. Deliberately. He'd set out to seduce her for the sole purpose of proving his grandfather's innocence. He'd known that she would be a casualty of his war with the Delanceys.

But as he'd made his plans to woo her and use her to find the proof he needed, he'd forgotten one very important thing. He'd forgotten that she was a real human being with real feelings and a heart that could be broken. Then, as he'd gotten to know her and discovered just how big and how open and pure her heart was, it had become harder and harder to convince himself that he was doing the right thing.

So here he was, and all he had to show for two months' effort was a nagging ache under his breastbone that felt as though it had been hurting forever.

And right now, the pain was getting worse. He rubbed his chest, but it didn't help.

He threw back the afghan and stepped out onto the balcony. It was raining and the heavy overcast blocked any sign of dawn or sunrise. The bridge and ship lights were pale and twinkling and haloed by the water droplets, just like Cara Lynn had described them. It did look like a wonderland.

Jack crossed his arms and rested against the facing of the French doors. He let his head fall back as he tried to figure out his next step. What now? Now that he'd screwed everything up?

Not only had he hurt Cara Lynn, he'd accidentally revealed himself and his true purpose, and thereby ruined his only chance to get a look at the letter she had. Convincing her to show him the letter had been his best chance—maybe his only chance to find out the truth about that day. Now he'd blown that chance by his own carelessness.

He still had the option of petitioning the court to retry the case based on DNA evidence, but his petition would probably be denied. Even if it was granted, the Delanceys would be notified, and they'd band together and use their influence to argue against reopening the case.

The hard truth was that without Lilibelle Guillame's last journal or the letter, all Jack had were his grandfather's letters, and he knew they didn't prove anything. At best they were a written statement as told by a witness and suspect. At worst, they were the lies of a convicted killer.

He couldn't petition the court until he had conclusive evidence that the wrong man had been convicted. There was no way he'd risk being turned down for lack of probable cause.

He straightened and looked out at the lights on the river again. He should have been more careful. He'd been arrogant and that arrogance had made him careless. In time, he could have convinced Cara Lynn to let him see the journal. She'd have let her husband, Jack Bush, see it. But she would never allow Armand Broussard's grandson to get his hands on it.

Now, if Jack wanted it, he'd have to steal it.

Chapter Six

When Jack left the balcony and went inside, it was a few minutes after six. He didn't know if Cara Lynn had to be up early or not, but she almost always rose by six-thirty or seven. If he was going to retrieve the letter and read it, he needed to do it now. The realization made him feel even worse. He was still deceiving her, still betraying her.

He was tempted to tiptoe down the hall and make sure she was still in bed and not in the shower or getting dressed. But she'd locked her door last night. He remembered the sound of the lock snicking deliberately and loudly into place.

If he paid attention, he should be able to hear her unlock the door. He could hide the letter until he had time to read it, then put it back before she ever realized he'd touched it. He'd just peel the cellophane tape the best he could and if she asked him about whether he'd opened it he'd deny any knowledge. After all, as much as he'd already deceived her, how much more could it hurt to deceive her a little more?

So, with merely a glance toward the bedroom doorway, he went into the pantry, knelt, moved the baseboard out of the way and reached inside for the letter.

It wasn't there.

He paused, stunned. It had been there yesterday and he'd put it back just exactly as he'd found it. So what had happened? Had Cara Lynn sneaked into the pantry and taken it during the few hours he'd slept, or while he'd been out on the balcony?

His pulse jumped at the idea that she'd taken the letter out of the envelope and read it. That meant he could read it with impunity, because it was now unsealed.

He reached a little farther inside, just in case the envelope had somehow gotten moved, but all he encountered was the roll of bills, the passport and the velvet necklace box that held the necklace. "Damn it," he whispered and reached for the piece of baseboard to put it back in place.

At that instant, he heard Cara Lynn coming into the kitchen. Cursing silently, he shoved the baseboard back into place, picked up a couple of bottles of sparkling water and rose.

Just as he came out of the pantry and back into the kitchen, acutely aware of the irony of being caught with water bottles in his hands, Cara Lynn opened the refrigerator door. When she heard him she turned, still holding onto the handle.

"What are you doing?" she asked, her gaze grazing his and moving on down to his hands.

"I was—"

"Really, Jack? Water? You're going to try my own

trick on me? Believe it or not, I'm smart enough to figure out what you were doing in there."

"What?" he said, knowing he was in big trouble. He
could feel his face getting hot, then hotter and he was
sure it was probably red as a firecracker. "What are
you talking about?"

"Don't insult my intelligence. I got the letter out last
night while you were asleep. Imagine my surprise when
I saw that the flap on the back was facing forward, when
I clearly remembered putting it in there front side out."
She took a breath. "What I can't figure out is how you
knew about the letter in the first place."

Jack shook his head, trying to keep his expression
neutral, but his face was burning now. He was so busted.
"Listen, you need to give me a chance to explain—"

Cara Lynn was so angry her ears had turned red.
Jack thought, better from anger than from excruciat-
ing embarrassment, like his.

"You keep saying that, Jack. I mean, *Jacques.* You
keep telling me to let you explain. But what do you
have to explain? It seems pretty straightforward to me.
It's the same old story. Boy woos girl, boy marries girl,
boy wants revenge instead of love, girl finds out, girl
divorces boy. What do you think, because I'm seeing a
major motion picture."

"Cara Lynn, stop talking for a minute, please."

But she couldn't. If she couldn't maintain the anger
and the sarcastic banter she'd start crying. She couldn't
explain to him that she'd known something was wrong
ever since the first time she'd met him. Granted, they'd
hardly been able to keep their hands off each other.

Granted, she'd been fascinated with him from the first moment she'd seen him. Then, when he'd asked her to leave with him, she'd abandoned her own gallery showing for him.

She'd fallen in love with him at first sight. Then, after their first night together, she'd known she could spend the rest of her life with him. She'd never met anyone so interesting and sweet and, she'd thought, so genuinely interested in her.

Then, poor deluded girl that she was, she'd married him.

"Don't tell me to stop talking," she snapped. "This is my apartment and you were trying to steal my letter."

"Okay, okay," he said, holding out his hands, palms turned down in a *let's calm down* gesture. "I didn't steal anything, so—"

"Only because I got to it first," she said.

"Listen, let's stop arguing for a minute, okay?"

"That wasn't arguing. I was stating a fact."

Jack shook his head and closed his eyes for a second. "Then, let's stop talking."

Cara Lynn glared at him. "And what, stand here and glare at each other?"

"No," Jack said, spreading his hands again. "We'll talk. But we'll be talking about a solution, not just yelling at each other."

She opened her mouth to make a sarcastic retort, but he was looking at her somberly. She closed her mouth, then took a deep breath to calm herself. "Okay. Go ahead. What's your solution?" She heard her voice take on a sarcastic twang and she winced. She had really tried to talk normally.

Jack had heard it, too, because his lips thinned and that tic started up in his jaw. He cleared his throat. "We both want the same thing—wait!" he put in hurriedly when Cara Lynn opened her mouth. "The truth. We both want the truth—right?"

Cara Lynn almost jumped in to say that she knew the truth, but she controlled herself. She literally bit her tongue as she nodded.

"What we're hoping is the truth is different for each of us, but we know that once the truth is proven, we'll both have to accept it. We'll have no choice."

She nodded again. Was he really going to propose some kind of rational compromise? And if so, why? So far, everything he'd done had been to further his own goal. Why would he change now?

Of course she knew the answer to that question, or at least she thought she did. He needed the information he thought might be in the letter, and he was willing to pretend to be cooperative in order to get it. She shook her head.

"What? You know I'm right. When we have proof of what really happened, one of us—hell, maybe both of us, are going to be crushed. But proof is proof."

"No," she said, still thinking about what he was trying to do. "No. All you're doing is trying to get a look at the letter, and I'm not about to let you get your hands on it. It's mine, and I can't think of a single reason why I'd let you see it."

"Whoa," he said, pushing the fingers of one hand

through his hair, leaving it slightly spiky. "I thought we were in agreement, and you're already refusing to share your information?"

Cara Lynn put her hands on her hips. "I'll share mine if you'll share yours."

Jack's gaze sharpened and his eyelids narrowed. "Mine? What do I have that you want?"

"I'm talking about what's in that briefcase that you can't seem to let out of your hands, much less out of your sight."

Jack didn't speak, but she could see the surprise in his eyes through his narrowed lids.

"Okay," she said. "Then we're right back where we were. We're stuck in a standoff. Neither one of us trusts the other, with good reason." She added the last three words under her breath, but Jack heard them. She saw his shoulders stiffen.

"I don't think we have any choice but to trust each other on this. Otherwise we'll be fighting all alone."

"All alone?"

"That's right," Jack said. "Look at us. We've been so close these past two months. And as long as we're searching for the truth, we're going to stay close—physically at least."

"Close." Cara Lynn laughed. "I disagree. I don't think we've been close at all. I think I've been deluding myself, ignoring the doubts I've had ever since I first met you. And I think you've spent every second of these two months deceiving me. Why would I even stay around you at all?"

He shrugged. "Because better the enemy you know than the one you don't know."

Better the enemy you know. Did she know him? Cara Lynn looked at the man she knew as Jack Bush. She barely knew him at all, and yet she knew him better than she did anyone else in the world. She knew every inch of that lean, hard body. She knew that his hair always smelled like soap and oranges. She knew that his skin was warm and kind of smooth and rough at the same time.

"Why would you say that?" she asked dully.

"Say what?"

"The enemy you know. I don't know you." She shrugged, throwing a hand up in a helpless, hopeless gesture. "I didn't even know your real name."

For a moment, he didn't say anything. He glanced down looking inward, she thought. Then he met her gaze again, and if she were able to trust her instincts, she'd think his eyes held sadness and regret.

"Oh, you know me," he muttered.

From somewhere deep within her came an almost overwhelming urge to smooth out the frown lines between his brows, but when she took a half step forward, it seemed to spur him into action.

He stepped backward, cleared his throat and nodded. "Okay, Cara, I'll show you some of my grandfather's letters from prison, starting with one of the first ones. But when I give you that letter, you give me your letter from your grandmother."

She was startled. "You don't know it's from my grandmother," she said.

"Come on," he sighed. "Who else would it be from? And you can stop the defensive posturing. We both know we're going to exchange letters. It's the only way we can be sure that we're both working toward the same goal."

He saw the resignation on her face that told him she'd acquiesced.

Five minutes later, he was sitting at the kitchen table, trying to decipher Lilibelle's beautiful handwriting. He had a pad and pen and was transcribing it as he read it.

"Damn," he muttered. "Can you tell what this says?"

When she didn't respond, he looked up to find her engrossed in his grandfather's letter. He'd chosen one that didn't mention Paul Guillame. From what he'd been able to gather, apparently no one knew that Paul had been at the fishing camp that day. He wanted to see if Cara Lynn noticed and asked about him.

He went back to her grandmother's letter, doing his best to make out the words, figuring he'd get her help with the indecipherable ones after she finished reading.

Once he'd gone through the entire two pages, he sat back and looked at what he had so far.

Dear Cara Lynn,
I am an old woman now. When I was your age, I never thought I'd grow old. Many's the _____ I wish I didn't. But I am here, veiny hands, _____ face. I _____ _____ choose someone to have my treasures. My sons want them, as do _____. If Robert Jr. had _____ _____, ___ _____.

So having _____ two _____ gifts to give, I choose you, the youngest. I shall _____ until you marry to give _____ the last journal. Not until you have a love of your own, can you know the joy and heartbreak ___ ___ _____ and then perhaps, ___ ___ understand why I did ___ ___ _____. My _____ is that you hide or _____ the journal, but I will be gone so _____ . Do _____ will with it. Nothing can _____ me any longer, and I do not _____ anything.

Ta Mémé, Lilibelle Guillame Delancey

20 Février 2001

Even with all the words he couldn't decipher, Jack was sure that Lilibelle's letter was her confession.

He sat back and watched Cara Lynn. She was bent over Papi's letter and seemed to be having as much trouble reading it as he'd had reading Lili's. But for her, penmanship was not the problem. Papi's words were written in neat block letters. It had to be the content that Cara Lynn was frowning over.

When, at long last, she looked up, he saw sadness and fear in her expression. For a long moment, the two of them stared at each other. Jack could read her thoughts as easily as if she'd spoken. She knew, just as he did, that each one of them held a document that could potentially destroy the Delancey family, if the words were true.

Alone, neither could be called evidence, but together they might be enough to convince a judge to reopen the case and allow DNA evidence to be presented, especially if the indecipherable words in Lili Guillame's letter said what Jack was sure they did. And Jack believed with all his heart that his grandfather's DNA would not be on the murder weapon. The police report he had indicated that there were two types of blood on the weapon, O positive and O negative. Con Delancey had O negative blood, while Lilibelle and his grandfather both had O positive.

But right now, he wasn't willing to share that much with Cara Lynn. He wasn't yet sure he could trust her. She hadn't promised him that she wouldn't go to her brothers. If she told them about the possibility of DNA testing, would they intercept and block his request?

Jack stood and stretched, then went around the table and opened the refrigerator door. "Want some water?" he asked.

"Hmm?"

He looked at her. She was still looking down at the letter in her hand. Obviously she hadn't heard him.

"Water?" he said again.

"Oh. Yes, please."

He set a bottle beside her and went back to his chair. As he sat, she reached for her grandmother's letter.

He snatched it up. "Hang on. I can't read everything. I want to take another look at it."

"No. I want it back," Cara Lynn said. "I don't want anything to happen to it."

"Hey," he said, holding it out of reach when she tried to take it again. "Watch out. I'll give it back to you when I'm done with it."

"I don't want it torn or wrinkled."

"Then stop grabbing for it. Come on, Cara Lynn, why would I want to destroy your grandmother's letter to you. It confirms what my grandfather said. He didn't kill Con Delancey. She did."

"What?" Cara Lynn snapped. "She does not say that."

"Oh, come on. She says right here, 'I shall wait until you marry to give you the last journal. Not until you have a love of your own, can you know the joy and heartbreak of love and then perhaps, you can understand why I did *something, something—*"

"Well *something* is not *kill my husband.*"

"No," Jack said. "But I think it says *did what I did* or *what I had to do.* Then she goes on to say, 'My hope is that you hide or *something* the journal, but I will be gone so it is yours. Do what you will with it. Nothing can *something* me any longer and I do not *something* anything.' I'm sure that's *nothing can hurt me* and *I do not regret anything.*"

"You don't know that. You said you couldn't read her writing."

"I can read it well enough to figure out what she's saying." He waved the letter. "You can't deny that this sounds like a confession."

Cara Lynn thumped the paper with her knuckles. "I can deny it all I want to. This isn't proof of anything. It's your grandfather's word against—against…hers. Now give me my letter," she said, folding his grandfather's letter and handing it back to him.

"In a minute. I want to ask you something first."

"Give me my letter!" she demanded, reaching for it.

"Cara, damn it, stop. If you want to get into a scuffle, I'll guarantee you I can take you. And if you think I won't because you're a girl, then keep grabbing at the letter."

She crossed her arms, leaned back in her chair and fixed him with a stony glare. "Fine. Go ahead."

He held onto the letter while he spoke. "I need you to promise me that you won't tell your family about all this."

She laughed. It was a short burst that had no humor in it. "Are you kidding me?" she said incredulously.

"No. I'm not kidding. I'm absolutely serious. If I'm going to trust you to work with me to find out the truth about who killed your grandfather, I've got to know you won't betray me to your family."

"Betray— You've got a lot of gall, asking me to promise you something like that."

"Oh, and I need to know if you've already told anybody and who they are. All of them."

"Who would I have told? I just found out."

"Not just. You found out yesterday morning, didn't you, when you came back by the apartment to change clothes and found my notepad," he said. "You've seen your mother since then, and who knows who else. You could have told all of them for all I know. And of course, you have a phone. You could have told the entire Delancey clan, hell—most of the city, by now."

"I—didn't," she said evenly, although how she made her voice even he didn't know. Because her expression was twisted into a mask of anger and something else he couldn't quite identify. Could it be hurt? Had he hurt her feelings?

"First of all, I've already promised not to reveal your 'true identity—'" she surrounded the two words with air quotes "—to any of my family.

"As for all this—" she gestured at his briefcase and the letter from his grandfather. "How can I talk to them about all this and not tell them about you? So I think I've covered that. Now, you have to promise me the same thing."

"The same thing?" he asked. "What do you mean?"

"I mean don't tell your family. And for sure as hell, don't tell my family."

Jack shook his head tiredly. "My *family* consists of my mom, who lives in Florida with her sister. Papi was my dad's father. So Mom cares nothing about all this. All she cares about is that her *murderer* father-in-law is finally dead. So you don't have to worry about my family." He heard the bitterness in his voice and was a little surprised. He'd never spent much time thinking about how his mother had reacted to his grandfather's imprisonment. His dad had already been sick at the time and died only a couple of years later. That was probably at least part of the reason that he, Jack, had been so close to his grandfather. Papi had filled the role of father for him.

He and his mom talked, and he visited her during the holidays, so he supposed they were as close as many mothers and sons. But, when his grandfather died, Jack had felt as though he'd lost his family. Maybe that was why clearing his grandfather's name was so important to him.

He just wished he'd started digging for the truth years before, instead of waiting until after Papi had died.

"Jack?" Cara Lynn said. "Will you promise?"

He shook his head sharply and blew out a frustrated breath. "Sure. I promise I won't tell my family."

"Or friends, or *my* family. I don't want my family upset for what's probably no reason."

"Or friends or your family," he repeated. "I solemnly swear."

"You don't have to be so sarcastic about it,"

"Sorry," he mumbled, sliding the sheet of fine parchment paper across the table to her. When she took it, he saw her fingers trembling. She carefully folded it and stuck it back into its fragile envelope. Then she rubbed her temple shakily. "Thanks," she said shortly. "Now, I've got a headache. I'm going to bed." She stood, gripping the back of her chair.

"What's the matter?" Jack asked.

She shook her head, then rubbed her temple again. "Nothing. I think I forgot to eat. I'll be fine."

"I could fix you a sandwich—"

Cara Lynn held up a hand, her expression pained. "Don't!" she said. "Don't start offering to do things for me. We may still have a marriage license binding us together, but as far as I'm concerned, you and I—" she pointed back and forth between them "—are *nothing*."

Chapter Seven

Paul was becoming desperate. He'd spent his entire adult life as caretaker of Claire Delancey's Garden District home, while she lived in France. He'd struck a deal with her to live there rent-free and care for, repair and renovate the beautiful but decaying old home.

Now Claire was dead and her will stated that her home and all current furnishings and décor would go, not to Paul, but to her newly found granddaughter, Hannah Martin. Suddenly, it occurred to Paul that he was about to be homeless.

It had only been a matter of a couple of months since Claire had told him she'd reconnected with her estranged daughter, who was dying from liver failure and waiting for a transplant. To Claire's surprise and delight, her daughter had a child—Hannah, who was twenty-six years old.

It had all come to light when Hannah witnessed a murder and fled to New Orleans to ask for help from her mother's best friend, and instead had met the best friend's son, MacEllis Griffin—one of Dawson's D&D Security investigators. The two of them had been instrumental in breaking up a drug distribution ring and rescuing Hannah's mother, who'd been kidnapped and left for dead.

At the time, Paul had been happy for Claire, not considering what her newfound family would mean to him. Somewhere along the line, while he'd been living on Claire's money and doing his favorite things— remodeling and redecorating, he'd lost track of what belonged to him and what did not.

Claire's lawyers hadn't mentioned her checking account on which he was signatory, but he knew it was only a matter of time before they'd get around to closing it. Luckily, he'd recently bought materials to overhaul the two-story porch that wrapped around the entire front of the house. He'd already made a deposit to his own account in the Cayman Islands.

He sat at the French Provincial writing table in Claire's master suite, comparing his bankbook from his Cayman account with Claire's household checking account. Beside the account book was the police scanner he liked to listen to. The night had been quiet, very few break-ins or domestic disputes, and nothing more serious than that. He turned it off and picked up his tumbler of bourbon and stared at the account book in front of him.

Over the past twenty-plus years, he'd spent every bit of the money Claire had given him in quarterly transfers. The issue, if the lawyers discovered it, was that less than half of Claire's money had gone into the house. The rest he'd spent on himself.

To Paul, that seemed perfectly reasonable, given that

in his opinion, redoing an entire twenty-five hundred square foot house from roof to foundation over a period of a couple of decades was a full-time job. However, he couldn't be sure that her lawyers and accountants would agree that a caretaker's personal expenses other than shelter over twenty years equaled approximately three million dollars. After all, that was only a hundred and fifty thousand a year.

Looking at his Cayman account balance, he was extraordinarily pleased with himself that he'd managed to pad material and labor expenses enough to sock away just over a million. Not a bad retirement, he thought, sipping bourbon, for a job well done.

Despite what the lawyers might suspect, he felt relatively confident that there was nothing they could prosecute him for. He and Claire had set up this arrangement verbally. And as quickly as possible, he'd switched their correspondence from telephone to email, so he had proof of what she had expected from him. He had saved every email she'd ever sent him, even the few where she'd requested explanations for what had seemed to her outrageous expenses.

Because, even when she complained, she still had stated over and over that she had expected him to spend money on the house and to compensate himself. Not only that, he had sent her photos of progress on specific projects, and he'd saved those emails, too.

Claire's death was extremely annoying. Paul knew he was going to be harassed by the accountants and lawyers, and forced to produce two decades of receipts and invoices and bank statements. And, once all that was over, he was probably going to have to leave New Orleans. And none of those were even his biggest problem.

What was feeding his panic was something much worse. Claire had sent Lilibelle Guillame's priceless tiara and her last and most revealing personal journal to Cara Lynn on the occasion of her marriage. And Paul knew that even if the lawyers or accountants found discrepancies in his record-keeping, his fiduciary indiscretions of the past twenty years couldn't hold a candle to what he had done twenty-eight years ago. If the truth about Con Delancey's death ever came out, the Delanceys would destroy him.

But every moment that he did not have the journal in his hands was another chance for someone to read it and find out what had really happened that fateful day, twenty-eight years ago.

He didn't have the journal, but he did have an important piece of information that he was pretty certain nobody else had, except the little princess, Cara Lynn. They were the only ones who knew there had been a letter in the box. And she had it.

Paul had seen her catch the white paper in her fingers just as the lights had gone out. He'd counted the seconds until the emergency generator kicked in and was looking directly at Cara Lynn when the lights turned on again. She was slipping the bit of white into her small evening clutch.

He couldn't swear that what he'd seen was a letter. But he would bet it was. It only made sense that Lili or Claire or both of them would write a note to accompany the gift. Whether it had been written by Lili or Claire, whether it was a long letter or a brief note, it could contain information harmful to him.

He had made plans from the beginning for getting into Cara Lynn's house on the pretense of helping her with her genealogy research. However, she'd already put him off several times, claiming she was too busy, so he was going to have to change his plans. One way or another, he had to get his hands on that letter—and soon.

Picking up his tumbler of bourbon, listening to the ice pinging against the sides of the glass, he walked over to the bed. He dropped his dressing gown and climbed under the covers, propping himself up against the headboard. As he sipped the whisky, he thought about the best way to get that letter.

Picking up his cell phone, he paged through his call log, looking for the name he'd called a few times before, when he'd needed help. As he watched the names slide by, he asked himself if he was confident that if he did this, he could keep Cara Lynn from being hurt.

He spotted the name and clicked on it.

CARA LYNN WOKE in the dark, her head pounding. She couldn't see. Someone had turned off the lights or covered the windows or blocked out the sun. It was hard to breathe, too. She tried to turn over and couldn't.

Her head was covered. Her nose was pressed into the mattress. She clawed at the covers, trying to loosen them so she could get a full breath.

She had a vague recollection of taking migraine medication and lying down. She must have gotten twisted in the covers. She rolled her head back on her neck—or tried to. But the covers were too tight.

Panic rose like bile in her throat and she sucked in air desperately. She struggled to tear her way out of the covers. She had to have air. Forcing her mouth open, she wheezed and sucked every molecule of oxygen she could into her lungs.

"Help—Jack!" she tried to scream. But no sound came out. She just wasted air. She got her arms under her and pushed, but something weighed her down. She couldn't get any purchase with her legs, either. This wasn't just twisted covers. She pushed against the weight again. This time she identified the source of the pressure. Something—a hand—on her head was pressing her face into the mattress.

"Who—? Get off me!" she mumbled against the mattress.

Then something cold and round pressed into the soft flesh of her neck.

"Shut up!" a gruff, muffled voice said.

Terror hit her chest like a fist, knocking what little air she had left from her lungs. "Can't—breathe!" she rasped. "—can't—"

"Shut! Up! And be still!" the voice said, but the hand on the back of her head let up—a little. Her lungs spasmed and her head pounded as she finally managed to gulp in enough air to stop the burning in her chest. She pushed with her arms again, an instinctive move to gain some control of her body, but the hand on the back of her head shoved her back down and her face was mashed against the bedclothes again. Then the cold heaviness against her neck pressed harder, deeper—so deep it hurt.

"Be still or I'll shoot you!"

Gun! Cara Lynn's pulse throbbed where the barrel of the gun pressed into her neck. That increased the pain in her head and she felt nauseated. "Let me up," she begged. "Who are—"

"Don't talk. Listen."

The voice echoed in her ears like the low, eerie growl of an alligator in the swamp at dusk.

She nodded as best as she could with the twin pressures of the man's hand on her head and the gun. Her nose and mouth were half pressed into the too-soft sheets, so that she still had to struggle to breathe, but at least she could get air in. "Please—" she gasped, "don't hurt me."

"Then *shut up* and listen. Where's the letter?"

"What?" Cara Lynn blurted. "The what?"

The gun jabbed her, sending screaming pain up the side of her head. "The letter you pulled out of the journal."

Something was odd about the voice. It sounded like the man was deliberately deepening it, making it more bass and gravelly. The intense pounding pain in her head kept her from thinking clearly, and the grating roughness of the voice made it hard to understand him. "Journal?" she said, trying to think through the pain.

The gun jabbed again. "The *letter*. That was in the journal."

"Oh," she said, finally putting his words together into sentences that made sense. The letter. Whoever he was, he'd been there, seen her slide the letter out from between the pages of the journal, just before the lights went out, or sticking it into her clutch as the lights came on. And then it hit her. It didn't matter what he'd seen. What mattered was that this was someone she knew. *Dear God!*

"'Oh' is right," he growled. "Where is it?"

The man's hand shifted on the back of her head, letting up on the pressure a little more. Enough so she could answer him. Then she realized that his hand was trembling. He was nervous. He wasn't some all-powerful monster. He was a man and he was not completely confident of what he was doing. She tried to lift her head and he pushed her face into the sheets again.

"Watch it!" he growled.

"Please—need to breathe." She hoped a direct appeal might help. But he wasn't buying it.

"Hah. You're not dying, at least not yet. You'll *know* when you're dying."

"I don't—"

She felt his knee come down on the middle of her back and his voice was suddenly right in her ear. "Don't even try it."

She shivered. "I don't know—"

"I swear to God, woman, I will shoot you. You have that letter and I want it, now!"

Cara Lynn felt the gun barrel trembling, and something wet—a drop of his sweat?—fall on the back of her neck. He wasn't just nervous. He was terrified. Maybe she could use that to get away from him.

She remembered hearing her brothers talk about

people who were inexperienced with guns and how dangerous they were. Their trembling hand might jerk, the finger they were already pressing too tightly against the trigger might spasm and *Boom!* Their victim was dead.

This man could shoot her without meaning to. He had her pinned down on the bed. His gun was pressed into her flesh. If he pulled the trigger, she would die instantly and the noise would be muffled by the mattress.

"Okay," she said, the fist of terror in her chest squeezing her heart. She had only one chance. She had to give him what he wanted. She took a breath, her chest heaving in a staccato rhythm with her racing pulse. Her head still screamed with pain, so much that she could barely think. She prayed to God that she was doing the right thing. That once she told the man what he wanted to know, he wouldn't kill her anyway.

"It's in the briefcase, by the door," she whispered.

"You better be telling me the truth," he said, his mouth still close enough to her ear that she could hear the tremolo in it. "Because you won't live through the day if you're lying."

The nausea that was pushing against the back of her throat began to increase, not helped by the heavy knee in her back. The pain in her head was a constant throbbing now. She couldn't remember when it hadn't hurt. It felt as though the gun's barrel rose and fell against her neck with each beat of her heart.

Then, the barrel jabbed again. She moaned.

"I'm going to get the briefcase and leave. If you move a muscle…" She felt him straighten, felt the pressure of his hand and the gun's barrel lessen. Immediately, without moving a muscle, she suddenly found it easier to breathe.

"I won't—" she gasped.

"If you make one noise, move one inch, I will come back in here and shoot you right in the heart. Do you understand?"

She moved her head slightly, nodding. "I swear I won't move."

"And if that letter isn't there, I'll come back here and shoot your husband and you in your sleep."

Bile burned her throat. She swallowed as nausea curled in her stomach and acrid saliva filled her mouth. "Please," she rasped. "I swear I won't move."

"Count five minutes—three hundred seconds— before you move," he said, letting go the pressure on her head.

The gun barrel stayed at her throat and she could feel the man's hand, hovering over the back of her skull, waiting—just waiting—for her slightest movement. Then he picked up a pillow and put it over her head.

A burst of sheer panic cut through her like a laser.

"Put your hands over the pillow, on the back of your head. Clasp your fingers."

She did what he said. Without her hands to hold her head and upper torso away from the sheets, her nose and mouth sank into the soft bedclothes again. She was back in the nightmare. No matter that her head was turned sideways, she still felt as though she were suffocating.

"Now what are you going to do?"

What had he said? The pain behind her eyes was so intense, the struggle for breath so all-consuming that she couldn't think. "Count?" she mumbled against the sheets. "Count to three hundred?"

"Three hundred seconds. *Seconds*. You'd better do it or you're dead."

The gun barrel shifted as the man's weight left the mattress. Almost as soon as his weight was gone, the gun barrel was back, but not at her throat. It now pressed against her hot, sore temple. She heard him pick up the bedside phone and jerk the cord out of the wall. "Where's your cell phone?" he growled, jabbing the gun into her sore temple.

"I—"

"Where!"

"I think it's on the foyer table."

"Three hundred seconds," he whispered in her ear.

She breathed through her open mouth as she felt the gun move away from her temple. The man stood watching her for a long time. She felt him there. His presence was heavy, ominous.

She lay still, doing her best to breathe silently so she could listen. She wanted to hear his footsteps backing out of the room. Wanted to hear him pick up the briefcase from the foyer floor. Wanted to hear the front door open and close.

She did not move a muscle. Tears filled her eyes and fell, soaking into the sheets and causing her nose to run, which made it even harder to breathe, but she lay still as a stone, just as she'd promised.

She heard him walking through her apartment. Heard him stop in the kitchen to rip that phone's cord out of the wall.

When she finally heard the front door close, every muscle in her body contracted, ready to vault up and run to the living room window to catch a glimpse of the ghoul who had touched her, held a gun to her head and threatened her life. But she couldn't move and she hadn't gotten to three hundred seconds yet. In her mind, he was still standing there, just waiting for her to disobey him, so he could shoot her.

She couldn't say how long she lay still, her head pounding, her limbs cramping, her throat burning with nausea. She could never remember afterwards how many times she'd counted to three hundred. She only knew that he'd told her he would kill her. And she believed him.

Chapter Eight

Jack was not happy with the St. Tammany Parish Sheriff's Office. They'd hauled in a suspect in the theft of the journal, based on two partial fingerprints they'd found on the surface of the tiara. Jack had expressed his surprise that the thief hadn't worn gloves, but the detective told him there were some jewel thieves who refused to use gloves to handle the jewels, claiming that even the thinnest gloves were clumsy and one couldn't afford to drop a piece that could be worth millions of dollars. The police had recovered the journal from the suspect's house.

Jack had asked for the journal, or at least photocopies of the pages inside. He'd told them he'd settle for one or two specific dates if that would make them feel better. He'd been summarily turned down. According to Detective Phillips, the journal was evidence and neither it nor any of its contents could be released until the evidence lab was finished with it.

At that moment, Jack wished he could call on the Delanceys. With five of them on the job, either in New Orleans or St. Tammany Parish, he was certain they could obtain photocopies. But he wasn't about to ask them. If he brought one of them in, at best he would be out, at worst he'd instantly become a suspect.

He'd considered getting a court order instead, but he would face the same problem with it. Within minutes the Delanceys would be alerted, and he'd be hit with so many delays and objections that he'd probably never see the book. So he had to resign himself to waiting, and hope that Cara Lynn didn't decide to ask her brothers or her cousins for help.

All he'd gleaned from his long and futile visit to the sheriff's office was one thin file folder that contained a scant two-page report on the suspect, a mildly successful second-story man named Drakos Rodino, known for his connections to jewelry fencing operations.

When he got inside and set his keys on the foyer table, he saw Cara Lynn's cell phone. It was lying face down on the table and its battery was missing. "Cara?" he called. "Where are you?"

She didn't answer.

"Cara, hon? Did you drop your phone? Where's the battery?" He reached for his briefcase, but it wasn't on the floor of the foyer where he kept it.

"Damn it," he muttered. "Cara Lynn, what the hell's going on? Where's my briefcase?" If she picked up the code for the lock by watching him open it and was snooping inside, reading his grandfather's letters…

He realized he was angry, much angrier than he probably should be, but damn it, he was tired and frustrated, and all he wanted to do was sit down and go through the meager report that he'd gotten from Detective Phillips.

He'd probably already heard every tidbit that was in the skinny folder from the detective, but still, he wanted to read the report himself.

He rubbed his face tiredly, thinking that none of that was true. He actually didn't want to read the report, or research the small-time thief on the internet, and he certainly didn't want to get into an argument with Cara about getting into his briefcase.

What he wanted to do, what he *really* wanted to do was take her in his arms and make sweet hot love with her for hours, until he'd managed to forget about his grandfather, her grandfather, the Delanceys—everything except the sweet scent of her, the sensual firmness of her skin, the thrilling sound of the quiet gasps that escaped her parted lips as she came, sometimes merely from his touch.

He shuddered and did his best to force his raging libido under control.

"Cara?" he called again, beginning to be worried. Where was she? It was after six o'clock. It had taken him most of the afternoon to get the meager two-page police report.

After a quick check of the kitchen and her office, he headed for the bedroom. The lights were off and all he could see was a small mound on her side of the bed. He turned on the hall light, not wanting to disturb her if she was asleep, but wanting to be sure what he saw was not just piled up covers.

In the light from the hall, he could see the curve of her hip under the covers and her hair, which was tangled and spread across the pillow. As he took off his tie and unbuttoned his shirt, he fantasized about crawling into bed with her.

It seemed like the best idea he'd ever had. He yearned to snuggle up behind her, forgetting that she'd snooped in his briefcase, forgetting that his hours at the sheriff's office had yielded almost nothing.

He'd settle for just lying there, napping together. Or maybe, if she was willing, they could make slow, sweet afternoon love, sleep a while and then have a late supper.

Then he remembered her saying she had a headache last night. That must be why she was in bed in the dark at this hour. It must have turned into a migraine. He stepped closer to the bed. "Cara, hon? You asleep?"

She didn't answer.

"Cara?" he said louder. "Do you know where my briefcase is? Do you have it in here?"

He heard a small sound from her.

"And what happened to your phone? Where's the battery? Did you drop it?"

He thought he heard a sob.

"Cara?" He stepped closer to the bed. "Is your head still hurting?"

She didn't say anything, just made that strangled sobbing sound again.

"Hon? Are you okay? Can I get you anything?"

She shook her head.

"Hon, talk to me. I'm not mad. Cara?" Worried, he reached out and touched her shoulder.

She jumped as if she'd been stung and whirled, putting her back against the headboard and clutching the covers to her with both hands. *"No!"* she cried, without opening her eyes. "I can't—" a sob cut off the word.

"What's the matter?"

She was shaking her head, her eyes open and staring.

"Wake up, hon." He approached her gingerly. "You're asleep. Wake up."

"J-Jack?" she stammered, then sobbed again. She looked at him—or toward him, her eyes still staring blankly. The pupils were completely dilated. He knew she didn't see him.

Jack's entire being went on red alert. "It's me. Come on, talk to me. Are you all right?" He reached for her, arms out.

"No!" she cried, scooting backward across the bed and nearly falling off on the other side. She stumbled as her feet touched the floor, then she backed up until she was against the wall.

Jack felt his hands shaking as he held them up and out in a nonthreatening gesture. He took two tentative steps toward her. "Hon, it's me, Jack. Wait—" he said when she stiffened, throwing her hands up defensively.

His worry turned to a sick fear. Her phone with no battery. His missing briefcase. What had happened here? "It's Jack. Cara—" he whispered brokenly. "Talk to me. Tell me what happened. Please. Are you hurt?" He could barely breathe against the fear that suddenly squeezed his chest.

She relaxed slightly, blinking. "Jack?" she said hesitantly.

"That's right. It's me."

"Oh." Her legs gave way and he lunged for her, barely

catching her before she collapsed to the floor. As soon as he got his arms around her to support her, she tried to stand up and started pushing him away.

"It's okay, sweetheart. I've got you. Let's sit down on the bed. Okay?"

She turned her face into the curve of his neck. "Jack, it's you." And then she started crying.

He got her onto the bed and sat down with his back against the headboard, then pulled her into his arms. He held her as she cried, doing his best not to think about what was wrong. But his best wasn't good enough. His brain whirled with all the awful things he could think of. She'd finally collapsed under the realization of what he'd done to her.

He thought about his briefcase missing and her phone sitting on the table with no battery. What had happened here?

He pulled her closer, hugging her, muttering nonsense words, for a long time. But finally, he was worried that she was hysterical or something and that she'd never stop crying. He pushed her away enough to look at her.

Then he saw a raw, red place on her left cheek. He looked closer. It looked like the friction burn basketball players get from sliding across the hardwood court. Then he saw a bright red circle on the side of her neck that was beginning to turn purple, like a fresh bruise. And there was another raw place on her chin.

Jack's jaw clenched and that squeezing pressure was back in his chest. Something awful had happened—to her. Someone had hurt her. He caught her by the arms, holding her still against her struggles and doing his best not to hurt her.

"Look at me," he said, trying to keep his voice soft and gentle although inside he felt like bellowing with rage—not at her, but at whoever had caused her to be so hurt and scared.

She blinked and looked at him, fear clouding her face, her breath coming in little sobs, her head jerking slightly with each sharp inhalation. Then she turned her head and strained against his grip. "Let me go," she said in a quiet, pleading voice.

It took all the willpower he had not to shake her and yell, *It's Jack. Please. I didn't do this! Don't look at me like that.* "Cara, it's me," he said softly. "Please, hon, please talk to me."

"J-Jack?" she stammered and this time her eyes focused on his face. "Jack? Oh…"

She reached for him and he pulled her close with a sharp inhalation that he would never admit was a sob. "Cara, Cara, shh," he said. "It's okay. I'm here. It's me. Don't be afraid."

She talked through the tears that began to fall and kept falling as she clutched at his shirt, holding onto him with tightly clenched fists and burrowing her face into his neck. "It was awful. I was asleep. My headache wouldn't go away and it was make—making me sick so I came home and went to b-b-bed."

Jack held her in the circle of his arms—not tightly. He let her decide how close she wanted to be to him. He listened, with his jaw aching from tension, with his head feeling like it was going to explode with rage, as she described what had happened.

"I wo-woke up and he was holding my head down and he—ow!" she cried, recoiling.

He realized he had closed his fist around her arm. "Oh, God, hon, I'm sorry." He had to relax. Had to be calm. He blew out a breath and forced himself to relax as he listened to her recount everything that happened.

"And he made me tell him where the letter was," she finished. "I'm so sorry."

"Shh. What are you talking about? You don't have anything to be sorry about," Jack murmured to her. "What about the letter?"

"He made me tell him. I had to. The only place I could think of was your briefcase. I told him…." She took a sobbing breath. "I think he took it."

"Listen to me a minute. This is very important. Did he mention the letter first or did you?"

She shook her head and air stirred by her hair cooled his skin beneath the tear-dampened material of his shirt. "No. I never said a word. He asked me where it was."

"That means—"

She pulled away and looked at him, her face blotched and red, her eyes swollen. "It means he was someone who was at my parents' house—" she winced and screwed up her face in revulsion "—someone I know." She shuddered.

He pulled her back into his arms. "Cara? I need to ask you—are you all right? He didn't—hurt you? I mean—he didn't—?"

She shook her head. "No," she said. "I thought he was

going to suffocate me or kill me, but no. Nothing else."
She pushed away from his embrace and wiped her face
with her hands, then pressed her fingertips to her lips
and shook her head. "I've never—nobody's ever—done
anything like that to me." She took a shaky breath. "He
could have shot me, Jack. He could have—"

"Shot!" he cried. Shock arrowed through him. "He
had a gun?" The round red bruise on her neck appeared
to be the imprint of the barrel of a handgun.

He pulled her close and pressed a kiss to the top of
her head. "I know, hon. I know. And I know how scared
you were. Thank God you're okay," he whispered. "Or
I'd have to kill him."

Cara Lynn continued to shiver. Jack pulled her closer.
They sat there like that for a long time. Jack was content
just to hold her. She'd been through a horrible experience, and of course it was his fault. He'd like to think
that if he'd been here, maybe they'd have that guy in
custody right now.

He had no idea how long they sat there, holding each
other, when Cara turned her head and kissed his neck.
"Thank you," she said softly. "I think I'm better now."

"You don't look like you're better. You're still trembling. Why don't you take a shower and I'll fix you
something to eat."

Her only answer was to burrow closer into his arms.

"Or I can sit here all night and hold you," he whispered in her ear. "Want to stay like this for a while
longer?"

She nodded, then shook her head. "I want a shower."

He stood up. "Come on. I'll help you to the bathroom."

"I'm not an invalid," she protested, although she had to admit to herself that Jack's attention and concern for her was going a long way toward draining away the horror of what she'd been through. So she let him put his hand around her waist and help her to the bathroom as if she were breakable. He started the shower and adjusted the water's temperature. Then he began unbuttoning her shirt.

"What are you doing?" she asked.

"Just helping you get undressed."

"I can do that by myself," she said, laying her hands on top of his.

Jack looked at her, his dark eyes smoldering as he finished the blouse and let it drop to the bathroom floor. "I know," he said.

"So, what are you—really doing?" Her breath hitched when he reached for the fastener on her skirt.

He held her gaze. His brow furrowed and his dark eyes looked sad. "I guess I'm trying to think of a way to wipe that horrible memory out of your head, and replace it with something more pleasant. But that of course, depends on your thinking my suggestion is pleasant—" his voice gave out when she reached for the zipper on his pants. "Wait—what are *you* doing?"

"Just helping you get undressed," she said with a small smile.

"So, you're feeling better?"

Cara Lynn didn't answer. She pushed his pants down, then stripped off her bra and panties and climbed into the shower, pulling Jack in with her. She sighed as the warm water hit her face and neck and cascaded down her body.

"Cara, are you sure?" he said.

She looked at his naked body through the steaming spray. "Oh, I'm sure," she said. "Now close the door. You're letting all the hot water out."

She manipulated the shower fixtures until a wide, hard spray beat down on both of them. She lifted her face to the hot water. Her body began to relax in the wet heat. The disgust and fear that had roiled up inside her when the man had touched her sluiced away down the drain.

Jack's hands slid across her shoulders and down her arms, dissolving the chill that had clung to her since the man had said he would kill her. Jack pulled her back against him and continued to caress her.

"Cara," he breathed. "Your skin feels like rose petals. Thick and soft and sweet and delicate. I love touching you. I love the feel of your skin against my hands, against my body."

Cara Lynn sighed. There was something to be said for pure physical attraction. She knew that he didn't love her like she loved him. But she did believe what he'd just told her. She believed that he loved touching her and making love with her. Although his touch was purely physical, as she struggled to forget her attacker's hand on the back of her head, his knee in her back and the gun barrel against her throat, she knew physical could be enough.

This painful sham of a marriage was teaching her a lot about herself. She'd never even considered that she'd find herself in a loveless marriage. Worse, she'd never dreamed she would choose to stay with someone who was using her. Her grandmother's fractured words from the letter came back to her. *I shall wait until you marry to give you the last journal. Not until you have a love of your own, can you know the joy and heartbreak of love and then perhaps, you can understand why I did _____ __ _____.*

Had her grandmother somehow known that years after she'd died, Cara Lynn would marry a man who would betray her?

The question hammered at her brain, again and again and again. Yet right now, as Jack's hands, hot and soothing as the shower's spray, caressed her skin, she was surprised to find that she didn't care what was driving him. Maybe all he wanted was proof that his grandfather was innocent. Maybe the only reason he was here with her now was to ensure that she considered him safer than the unknown. She didn't care. She needed him, so she would accept whatever he chose to give her and she would give him back all she could.

"Cara?"

"Hmm?" she said.

He touched her forehead and her neck, then he touched the curve where her neck and shoulder met. "What's this?"

"Ow. I don't know. It stings a little. What does it look like?"

She felt him run a fingertip over the sore place.

"Tiny scratches," he said.

"I don't know," she answered dismissively as she moved to stand behind him.

"Hey, where're you going?" he asked, with a little chuckle as she slipped away from his caressing fingers.

"I'm right here," she murmured. She filled her hands with citrus-scented body wash and from behind him, massaged it into his muscular shoulders as the water flowed in rivulets down his honed, planed body. His biceps were as hard and smooth as river-worn rocks. His torso was a sleek, taut landscape. As she lay her cheek against his back and reached around to spread soap over his pecs, his abs and lower, she heard a sexy growling sound from deep in his throat.

He turned to her, his skin golden and glistening. He smiled at her and pushed wet strands of hair out of her face.

Cara Lynn stared. It was *that* smile. That wonderful, secret smile she'd thought she might never see again. If she saw it ten thousand times, she'd still be knocked out by it. He hadn't smiled at her like that since they'd gotten married. But right now, it was there on his face and no matter what else he was, she knew he would protect her.

She kept spreading the suds across his skin, her fingers delighting in the sleek hardness of his body. As she caressed him he put his hands on top of hers and followed her path, breathing hard, gasping when she finally moved her palms down to touch his arousal.

"Ah, careful hon," he muttered. Then he lifted her hands and slid his palms across hers, taking the liquid soap from her hands and using it on her body.

He rubbed her all over, encircling her breasts, rubbing his thumbs across her peaked, throbbing nipples. He slid his hands down her belly, pressing it, shaping it, then, ignoring her gasps and moans, he moved lower. She almost collapsed as he slid his hands between her thighs. "Jack—" she cried, catching onto his slick shoulders for balance. "Please—"

He stopped. "Enough with the soap," he murmured, aiming the showerhead lower, so that the strong spray hit her shoulders and his chest. Then he stepped into the path of the spray and turned around to rinse all the soap off his body.

"Rinse," he said. "I'll be outside." And he was gone in a small whirlwind of cool air.

Cara Lynn had no idea what he was doing. The first thing that popped into her head was that he'd abandoned her. He had brought her almost to the pinnacle and then he'd left her alone. As she rinsed the soap from her body, she touched where he had touched and the fading sensations made her want to cry.

When the soap was gone, she stepped out of the shower and into the folds of a large white towel that Jack held up for her. As he wrapped her in the fluffy warmth, his arms lingering around her in a protective embrace, she began to cry.

Jack stopped rubbing the towel over her body and caught her up in it, holding her close as he stared down into her face. "Cara? Did I hurt you?"

She wanted to scream *yes. Of course you hurt me. I almost died of the pain when I found out who you really were.*

But she didn't. All she did was collapse in his arms and let him guide her to the bed.

To her surprise and gratefulness, he'd stripped and remade the bed while she was rinsing off the soap. He lowered her gently down onto the blankets and rose above her. Then he was in her, filling her with his gentle strength and his heat. And it was enough—almost.

She ran her hands down his body, cool now from the water that had dried on his skin, over his corded muscles, his lean flanks, his hard, long thighs. When he began to move in her, her body, as always, slipped into his rhythm. Her breasts ached with it, her belly quivered, her loins burned. And tears still slid from her eyes.

Jack lifted his head and gazed down at her, that smile seeming unsteady, his lips quivering. Then he kissed her. As he did, his movements quickened, and Cara Lynn's entire being spasmed with delicious pleasure. Nothing he had done so far—nothing—made her feel like his kiss did.

When he kissed her, she felt everything. She felt his desire, so hot and swelling that he seemed ready to explode. She felt her own, climbing, climbing—so close, so very close.

Incredibly, they reached their separate peaks together, and for an instant Cara Lynn thought they might have exploded, the shock of their shared climax was that great. Then Jack collapsed beside her, his chest heaving, his breaths fast and uneven.

She lay, reveling in the fading sensations, loving the small spasms she felt from Jack's body that told her he was basking in the afterglow of their lovemaking, just as she was.

He turned his head toward her and she met his gaze. He smiled at her again—that same smile—and a thrill arrowed through her. Then, to her utter surprise and delight, he lifted his head and kissed her full on the mouth. It wasn't a hesitant kiss, or a desperate one. It was languid, sweet and yet erotic, and it was long. When he finally pulled away, his eyes were troubled. "Cara?" he said.

"Oh, Jack," she said, pressing her face into the hollow of his shoulder. "I love you."

Every muscle in his body went rigid. Only then did she realize that she'd said those words aloud. She didn't move as she waited to see what he would do.

In the weeks they'd known each other, she'd never said it before. She'd waited, wanting him to say it first. But he never had. He'd told her all the things about her that he loved. He'd told her that he loved how she made love with him. He'd told her a lot of things. Specific things.

But he'd never once said the words *I love you* to her.

He lifted himself up onto one elbow and looked down at her as if he'd seen her on the street and stopped, trying to figure out if he knew her. It was a detached, hurtful look. He took a deep breath.

"I'm sorry." he said. Then he turned away and left their bed.

Chapter Nine

While Cara Lynn was drying her hair and pretending the wetness on her cheeks wasn't tears, she smelled the most wonderful aroma. When she came into the kitchen, she found Jack making an omelet and perking coffee.

"Hey," he said. "You hungry?"

"I didn't think so, but that coffee and those eggs smell great. I didn't know you could cook."

He glanced at her sidelong. "I don't give up my secrets easily."

"No," she responded wryly. "You don't."

Jack didn't speak for a few moments as he finished cooking the omelet. "I found a couple of English muffins in the freezer. How do you want them? Toasted and buttered?"

"Mmm. Yes."

Once they were seated and eating, Jack looked up at Cara Lynn. "I didn't ask you if you wanted to call the police," he said. "I probably shouldn't have let you take a shower."

She shook her head as soon as he said *police*. "No. I don't want to call them."

"Are you sure, because if you need to—?"

"I'm absolutely sure," she snapped, then frowned at him. "If I call them, I'll have to tell them what he was after." She shivered and chafed her arms. "Do you think I should?"

"It's not about me," he said. "You're the one who was attacked. You're the one who could have been hurt or killed."

She nodded as a faint echo of terror shook her. "I know, and trust me, I'm from a family of cops. I know how important it is to call the police! But you know what's going to happen if I do. My family will be pulled right into the middle of all this, and you and I will have to tell everybody everything. Are you ready to do that? I mean, are you ready to expose yourself that way?"

Jack set his fork down with a clatter and took a swig of coffee. "You're awfully anxious all of a sudden to protect my information. I mean, you've wanted to let your brothers and your cousins in on this from the beginning. I don't know why you're even hesitating."

She shrugged as she speared the last bit of omelet. Then she sat back in her chair and sipped her coffee. "I did want to tell them. But for one thing, I don't know for sure that you'd have made it this far alive if they'd known what you did. And for another, I guess you successfully convinced me that I don't want them to know I let myself be duped by a Lothario."

Jack's expression tightened. He didn't wince—not exactly, but she saw right away that he didn't like being called that.

"Now you're the one wanting to call the police. I'm confused. Not that confusion is a brand new state for me."

Jack's face changed again. It seemed to go dark, as if a cloud had passed over the sun. "I don't like the fact that you were attacked by a dangerous man with a gun, who bruised you and threatened your life."

She set her cup down. "Well, neither do I." She spread her hands. "So now you're all about protecting me. Well, sorry if I'm just a little skeptical. It's still about finding proof of your grandfather's innocence, isn't it? Are you trying to use some kind of reverse psychology on me? Like you know if you want me to tell the police I'll dig my heels in and refuse? And then of course you'll look good because you were trying to get me to call them."

Jack raised his eyebrows and grinned at her. "That's a little bit of a stretch, don't you think?" he asked. "If you don't want to call them, that's your decision I guess. But why not?"

Cara Lynn got up and put her dishes in the sink and turned on the hot water. She picked up the dish brush and washed her plate, cup and fork.

Jack came up and reached around her to set his dishes down. "Wash mine, too?"

Without speaking, she quickly washed his and set them in the dish drainer. When she dried her hands and turned around, he didn't move backward. He stood his ground and stared down at her. "What is it you don't want the police to know, Cara?"

She shrugged, but he placed his forefinger under her

chin and lifted it so she was looking at him. "What? Was there something else with that letter?"

She thought she was holding her gaze steady, but he saw something in her eyes. When she started to shake her head, he held it still. "There was. Okay, spill it. We promised to tell each other everything."

"We did not! And besides, you've already violated that promise, which—which we didn't make anyway."

"Your logic has more twists than a pretzel, hon. What else was in the envelope?"

She ducked and slid away from him. "Why should I tell you anything else?"

Jack assessed her. "If you do, and if it's important enough, I'll tell you something I haven't told you yet."

"See!" she cried, throwing the dish towel down. "I *knew* you hadn't told me everything. What? What is it you've kept a secret? Is it something about my grandfather?"

"Oh, no. Ladies first. You tell me yours and *then* I'll tell you mine."

Cara Lynn studied him. "I don't think you've got anything."

"Oh, I've got something. It's a big something, too. Huge. It *could* give me the proof I need."

That she believed, because his dark eyes were glittering with excitement. Whatever he had, he was placing a lot of hope in. What he didn't know was that her secret could give him the proof he needed, too, or at least put him on the right track. And that was Cara Lynn's dilemma. Could she just hand him an important piece of the puzzle he was looking for? The puzzle that could easily rip her family's hearts out? "Okay, well if that's the case, then, you certainly don't need anything I've got. You're ready to go, right?"

Jack's eyes lost a bit of their shine. "I actually do need one thing, in order to—" He stopped himself and shrugged. "But I'll get it. You just sit back and watch. I'll get the proof I need, because it *is* out there."

"Okay, then," she said, glancing at the clock over the sink. "I've had a long and horrible day, so I think I'm going to go to bed early."

"Cara? Answer one more question for me. Why are you so sure you know the man who attacked you?"

She turned back to look at him. "Because he knew about the letter."

Jack nodded, crossing his arms and leaning against the refrigerator. "And how could he know about the letter?"

"Because he was there and saw it?" she ventured.

Jack shook his head. "I don't know. Nobody else saw it. I didn't. I wouldn't have suspected a letter if it hadn't been for that scrap of paper you dropped." He studied her for a moment. "What about your mom?"

Cara Lynn frowned. "What about her?"

"Had she seen inside the box before it was opened at the reception? Your mom doesn't seem like the type of person who would stage something that dramatic without checking out everything ahead of time."

She smiled. "You're right about that, but apparently, my grandmother gave Aunt Claire specific instructions about how she wanted the presentation made, and that included putting the items in a lockbox, just like we saw them, and putting the lockbox in a safe deposit box until I got married."

"So when the box was opened by that banker guy at the reception—"

"My mother said the box was sealed and the reception was the first time it had been opened since my grandmother gave the journal and the tiara to Aunt Claire."

"It's been here, in the bank, all these years?"

Cara Lynn nodded. "What are you trying to figure out?" she asked. "Whoever attacked me had to have seen me slip the letter into my purse. But if he saw it, then a bunch of people must have."

"No. They didn't. I didn't see it. It's a stone-cold cinch that your brothers didn't see it or we'd know about it. And I haven't heard a single person talking about it. Have you?"

He didn't wait for her answer. "I think anyone who'd seen the envelope would have been asking about it and questioning whether the envelope had been taken by the thief along with the journal and tiara."

"You're right about that. So nobody saw the letter except the thief and me."

Jack's gaze slipped away from hers and focused on something far away. He shook his head. "Right. The thief had to be somebody close."

"That's what I meant. Everybody there was family or friends, so whoever did this has got to be somebody I know."

"I'm talking about position. He had to be close enough to see what you did."

"Well, whoever he is, he has the letter now."

"No he doesn't," Jack said.

"What?"

"The letter's not in the briefcase. I gave it to the lawyer."

"Oh," she said. "Well, good."

Jack's face was somber as he looked at her. "Yeah. I think it was good. If the attacker had known the letter was not in the briefcase—"

"What?" Cara Lynn's stomach sank.

"He might have tried to get you to tell him where it was."

"Oh," she said.

Jack put his hand on hers. "I shouldn't have said anything. Don't worry. He's gone now."

She nodded doubtfully. "But now he still doesn't have it."

"True. But I don't think he'll try breaking in again. For all he knows, we've called the police." He reached out and almost touched her cheek before he checked his movement and pulled his hand back.

His aborted gesture reminded her of what he'd said earlier, in their bed. "Jack? Why did you say what you did earlier?"

"Hmm?" he said, his brows furrowing in a small frown. "What did I say?"

She shook her head and sighed. "Nothing. I'm tired. I've got to get some sleep."

"Yeah," he said. "I've got work to do— Oh, hell! I don't have my briefcase."

Cara Lynn stepped across the threshold from the

kitchen to the hall, stared down the long, unlighted corridor for a second, then turned back. "Jack?" she said.

His face showed his frustration at not having his briefcase. "What?" he answered shortly.

She paused. "Never mind. Good night."

She forced herself to walk down the hall to their bedroom. As she climbed into bed, she remembered. Jack had changed the sheets. Grateful tears gathered in her eyes as she slipped under the clean, crisp, freshly washed covers.

She turned out the bedside lamp and closed her eyes, trying to blot out the bad memories. She'd almost drifted off to sleep when she felt Jack's weight on the bed, and then his warm, strong body spooned her. He wrapped an arm around her and pulled her close.

"Oh," she sighed. "I thought you had to work."

"I do. I'd left my drawings on the coffee table where I'd been going over them yesterday, but I thought I'd lie here with you until you fall asleep."

Cara Lynn snuggled back against him and closed her eyes. She sighed, thinking there was nowhere in the world she'd rather be than spooned against the very obviously aroused body of her husband, who loved her.

But that wasn't where she was. She was in bed with her husband, but he didn't love her. And as soon as he got what he wanted from her, he'd be gone.

CARA LYNN SPENT the next morning at her studio. She'd been sketching a new piece. It was to be a large wall hanging, predominantly black and spiraling out from the center. In each spiral, she wanted to add more and more colors to the black, until the outer edges were brightly colored and nothing was left of the black except a meager background.

It was her interpretation of Jack's dark, dark eyes when he was angry or excited or turned on. Privately, she called it *His Eyes,* but she couldn't call it that. Not now. Maybe not ever.

After a few hours' work, she quit, frustrated. Her mind kept wandering back to the journal, and what her grandmother might have been scribbling so furiously in it on that fateful day.

On her way back to her apartment, she called her cousin Ryker, who worked at the St. Tammany Parish Sheriff's Office as a detective.

"Hi, Cara Lynn, are you feeling better?"

For an instant, Cara Lynn thought Ryker was talking about the attack of the day before, that neither she nor Jack had told anyone about. "I'm—I'm—" she stammered.

"What's wrong, kiddo? That bump on your head confusing you?"

"Oh," she said. *Bump on the head.* Of course. He was asking about the night of the reception. "The bump. I forget about it until I look in the mirror and see the little cut or absently touch my forehead. I'm doing fine," she said, hearing in her own ears how nervous and deceptive she sounded.

"Okay," Ryker said, a tinge of doubt in his voice. "What can I do for you? Did you remember something?"

"No. Nothing like that. I wanted to ask you a favor."

She heard a rustling of clothes that sounded like he was sitting up straight.

"What is it?" he asked.

"Is there any way you could get me copies of a couple pages from Grandmother's journal? Or—do you know how long they're going to keep it? There's some information I need for my genealogy research."

"That journal is evidence in your case right now. So the timing couldn't be worse. Can't you work on something else until the crime lab's done with it? You'll get it back."

"I'm afraid it could be years. And I thought maybe right now, before trial starts, it might be easier to get a little leeway. Ryker, this is really important or I wouldn't ask. I feel like I can't move forward until I get it."

"What's going on, Cara Lynn? By now you should have piles of papers and documents and letters to work with. The journal can wait."

"But Ryker—"

Ryker sighed. "What pages?" he asked.

"I don't know the page numbers," Cara Lynn said, a bit hesitantly, "but I do know the date. It's the day our grandfather was killed."

"What?" Ryker sounded genuinely shocked. "The day—? What do you need that for?"

Cara Lynn pushed her left hand through her hair. She was finding it easier to lie these days. What did that say about her, much less about her sham of a marriage? "I'm working on Grandmother's side, the Guillame side of the family," she said. "And I feel like I need the whole thing, but under the circumstances, I'll take whatever I can get. Maybe I'll have enough information to estimate the number of pages I'll need to put aside for that section."

"I'll see what I can do, but the detective in charge of the case, Charlie Phillips, is not very fond of me."

"What about Reilly or Lucas?"

"My twin brother? Charlie's not too happy with him, either. Reilly and I were instrumental in proving that his partner, Dagewood, had killed Reilly's wife's sister several years ago. Phillips has never forgiven us. I don't think he knows Lucas, but I doubt he'll be thrilled with any of the Delanceys."

"I'm sorry. Is there anything—?"

"I'll see what I can do, but don't get your hopes up too high."

"Oh, Ryker. Thanks!"

JACK HADN'T MEANT to be so late getting back to the apartment, but after going by the police station and being put off yet again by Detective Phillips, he'd driven over to Biloxi to take care of some personal business. At his own apartment on Biloxi's Back Bay, he picked up copies of his grandfather's letters, then he swung by the landlord's apartment to pick up any mail and packages that had been delivered, and while he was there, he went ahead and paid the next three months' rent.

Then, on his way home, he went by the police station again, and what Detective Phillips told him that time made him furious. He drove home with his hands white-knuckled on the steering wheel and his brain whirling with everything he wanted to say—no, *shout* at Cara Lynn.

So when he burst into the house and found her in the kitchen cooking jambalaya, the little domestic scene sent his anger spiraling out of control.

"Hi?" she said, glancing over her shoulder at him with a smile as she stirred. When she met his glare, her smile faded. "What's wrong?"

"Have you got no sense whatsoever?" he yelled, throwing his mail and the file folder down on the kitchen table.

Cara Lynn frowned at him, blinked a couple of times, then said, "I'm fine, thank you. You don't seem to be doing so well."

"Stop it!" he cried. "Just stop it. What the hell were you thinking, going to your cousin about the journal?"

She frowned. "How do you know—"

"I know because I went by there this afternoon to see if Detective Phillips, who is *in charge* of the investigation, *not* your cousin, had decided to allow me to see the journal."

"He was going to let you see it? And you didn't tell me?"

"No, he wasn't going to let me see it, at least not any time soon. He was just stringing me along so I'd be cooperative. He might have eventually allowed me to read a page or two, depending on how he was feeling and how well the case was going. And depending on how cooperative I was being until he decided what to do about me." Jack huffed. "But now—"

"Now what? I didn't do anything different from what

you did. I called Ryker and asked him if I could see certain pages. I told him I was working on the genealogy and needed to look at a few pages around the date that our grandfather died, because I thought that Grandmother's handwritten notes might give me some insight into what happened that day."

"That's the problem! How could you possibly think that siccing a Delancey on Detective Phillips, whom I understand hasn't been too fond of the Delancey twins since they proved that his partner was guilty of murder a few years ago, was a good idea?"

Cara Lynn glared at him, her hands propped on her hips. "You didn't tell me you were trying to get a look at the pages."

"I told you I was going to the police station to see if I could get any new information. What did you think that meant?"

"How should I know!" Cara Lynn shot back at him. "So, did Phillips give you anything?"

Jack suddenly felt deflated. "No. What about you?"

She shrugged. "Ryker said he'd see what he could do, but he wasn't very encouraging. Do you want some jambalaya?"

"Yeah, please. It smells great," he said, abandoning his argument for the moment, because he really was hungry. "Anything I can do? Pour some wine?"

Cara Lynn shook her head. "Sit down."

Jack sat and flipped through his junk mail and flyers, and tossed them into a pile next to him. He started to open the folder Phillips had given him, but Cara Lynn set a plate of rice and shrimp and sausage in front of him. She poured two glasses of chardonnay, then sat down next to him.

"This is great," Jack said around a mouthful of rice. "What kind is it?"

"What kind?" she repeated. "Oh, you mean like a brand. I made it from scratch."

He glanced up at her. "Impressive. What's the occasion?"

She shook her head. "I got frustrated with my current fiber-art piece, so decided I'd cook."

He nodded. "Thanks."

She sent him a little smile as she started in on her plate.

Jack ate a few bites, watching her the whole time.

"Why are you staring at me?" she asked, reaching for her wine.

"Not staring. I'm—" he paused "—sorry about earlier."

"The screaming fit?"

He winced and nodded briefly in acknowledgement. "It's just that if your brothers find out what I'm doing, I'll lose—" He cut himself off. *Lose everything.*

What the hell was wrong with him? He couldn't say things like that to her. He might as well just flay himself open and invite her to eviscerate him. He'd be better off just packing his bags and forgetting his doomed quixotic dream to clear his grandfather's name.

In fact, when he'd walked into his apartment in Biloxi that afternoon, he'd felt an almost overwhelming urge just to close and lock the door and pretend he'd never even heard of the Delanceys.

But he knew that wasn't an option. Unfortunately, there was more at stake now than there had been when he'd first cooked up this harebrained scheme.

"You'll what?" Cara Lynn said. "Lose—?" Her gaze narrowed and a small furrow appeared between her brows.

"Nothing," he said, standing and taking his plate and glass to the sink. "Forget it. I'll do the dishes."

She tossed back the last of her wine, then stood as well, picking up her plate. "Thanks. I'll put the food away." She gestured back toward the table with her elbow. "What's in the folder?"

"I ran over to Biloxi and got copies I'd made of my grandfather's letters," he said as he rinsed the dishes and put them in the dishwasher.

She was quiet as she put the food away and wiped off the table. She picked up the bottle of wine. "We almost finished this," she said. "Want the last of it?"

He shook his head. "You go ahead."

She held up the bottle to the light to measure what was left. "Not even half a glass. I don't need any more after that migraine yesterday." She tossed the bottle into the trash.

Jack dried his hands. "Are you okay?"

She nodded, then turned the nod into a shake of her head. "I can't stop thinking about that man."

He heard the stress in her voice. "I get it, but you need to try. You'll just drive yourself nuts if you dwell on him. Trust me, he's not worth it, whoever he is."

She shuddered. "Maybe not, but there's something…

I can't quite figure it out. It's stuck right at the edge of my mind."

"What is?" Jack asked.

"I'm not sure. I think it's something about the man. I didn't recognize anything familiar about him, but then my head was buried in the pillow." She took a long breath as if still suffocating. "Ugh. I can't put it into words. It's right there, you know?" She held her hand out about three or four inches from her temple and wiggled her fingers. "That close."

"Sleep on it. Maybe you'll know in the morning."

Cara Lynn shook her head. "I slept on it last night, but I sure didn't know anything this morning." She sighed. "It's after nine. I think I'll lie down and read for a while. My head still feels strange." She started for the bedroom, then stopped. "By the way, I got a new battery for my phone and there was a message on it from Reilly. We're invited for drinks and hors d'oeuvres at their house. I have it on good authority that he and Christy are going to announce that they're pregnant."

"I don't think I'll go," Jack said.

"Oh, no. You're not bailing on me," Cara Lynn insisted. "You will go. You married the Delanceys when you married me, no matter what the reason was, and you will show up for at least some of the family events until you—" She paused for a beat. "We turned down my mother the evening of the gallery opening and so we need to go to this."

"You turned her down."

She lifted her chin. "With good reason. We should

leave here around six o'clock." She turned to head for the bedroom again.

"Cara?" Jack said.

"What?" She stopped.

"Thanks."

She looked at him. "For what?"

"For dinner. For—" he shrugged and felt his cheeks warm.

She stood still for a few seconds, then turned around. "Jack, sit down."

"What? Why?" he asked.

"Please," she said. "I need to show you something."

He pulled out a chair. "What is it?" he started, but she shushed him.

"Jack, please just wait, okay? This is not going to be easy." She walked to the foyer and picked up her purse, then came back and sat at the table. She opened her purse and retrieved a folded piece of thick blue paper from an inside pocket.

She set her purse on the floor and unfolded the piece of paper and just looked at it for a moment, her lips compressed. At one point the fingers of her right hand tightened where they were holding the edge of the sheet. Jack saw her knuckles whiten.

He had a strong feeling he knew exactly what she was holding. It was killing him not to just reach out and take it from her, but he restrained himself. He felt as if he were watching a feral kitten. He didn't want to move suddenly or do anything that would make Cara Lynn change her mind about what she had to show him.

If that piece of paper was what he thought it was,

then he couldn't blame her for hesitating. She could very well be holding the tool he needed to clear his grandfather's name.

It occurred to him that if she gave it to him, she'd also be giving him his ticket out. She'd be saying, in effect, *I know that as soon as you use this and manage to clear your grandfather's name, you have no further use for me, nor I for you.*

Was that true? Was he ready to leave, once the truth came out?

Chapter Ten

The truth.

Suddenly, he realized that not only was he assuming that the sheet of paper contained the truth, he was also assuming that it was going to contain *his* truth. It only made sense considering Cara Lynn's hesitation. If it stated that Armand Broussard was guilty, why would she hesitate? That would be good news for her family and a punch in the gut for him.

He forced himself to curl his hands into fists and keep them at his sides while he waited for her to either give him the paper or fold it up and say *Never mind*.

She folded the sheet, which sent his pulse racing, then held it in her left hand and tapped her right knuckles with it. Finally she looked up at him and he saw tears glistening in her eyes. For herself or for him?

"I know this is the right thing to do," she said, "but I hope you realize it's not an easy decision for me. In fact it totally sucks." She threw the paper down on the table in front of her, then interlaced her fingers and pressed her clasped hands to her lips.

"Are you—?" he started, then found he had to take a

breath before he could finish what he was saying. "Are you sure, Cara?"

"Oh, damn it!" she cried. "Take the thing and read it before I change my mind." She vaulted up, sending her metal dining room chair screeching across the floor, and went to the refrigerator and took out a bottle of sparkling water.

Jack's mouth was so dry he wasn't sure he could swallow, but he wasn't going to ask her to give him something to drink. In fact he wasn't planning to move a muscle until he'd read everything on that piece of paper. He unfolded it and for a moment, he felt as though he couldn't see anything. His vision was blurred. It took a few blinks before everything became clear. He blinked again and focused on the handwritten words on the sheet.

Dear Cara Lynn,

Somehow, when you're young, you never believe these days that you fear will ever come. I certainly didn't. It was only a few months ago, when my beloved Ivan died, that I actually believed that death was real. I was so lucky to have him for all these years.

Your mother wrote me that you've gotten married and sent me a snapshot of you and your husband, and has requested the items your grandmother left you.

Lilibelle wrote a holographic will after Con's death, specifying her wishes that you receive her two most precious items, but only after you were married. If I can, I'll be there soon after the reception at which you're reading this. I wish I could be there to celebrate with you, but as you may know, my beautiful granddaughter Hannah and her fiancé, Mack, have been here in Paris, visiting with me. I would love to see my daughter as well, but neither she nor I can travel right now. I hope to be able to see her after she recovers from her liver transplant.

Lilibelle was always my best friend. When she told me her secret and asked me to keep it, I had no choice but to follow her wishes. You will find, in her journal, her confession that she, not Armand Broussard, killed your grandfather, her husband. She couldn't bear the humiliation of him running for governor while he lived with his mistress, Kit Powers. I have not read the journal. I only read her letter to you and the note she wrote me. She wants you to read the entire journal, then make up your own mind what to do with the information.

Cara Lynn, I know you'll carefully study and assess everything you have just received and will do the right thing. I don't know what made her choose your marriage as the statute of limitations on this information, but I suppose she knew what she was doing.

Now, back to the photo of you and your new husband. He is quite handsome. As I...

JACK AUTOMATICALLY TURNED the sheet of paper over, but there was no writing on the back. He looked up and caught a look on Cara Lynn's face that he'd never seen before. When he met her gaze, she gave him a sheepish shrug. "There's another page," he said.

She nodded. "There is. But you have everything you wanted, right there."

"But she was talking about me."

"Just because it may be about you doesn't give you the right to see it."

Jack turned the sheet back over and read the entire page again. When he came to the part that said, point blank, that Lilibelle had killed Con, he read the words over and over.

You will find, in her journal, her confession that she, not Armand Broussard, killed your grandfather, her husband.

Each time Jack looked at those words, his heart rate sped up another fraction of a second. And to be perfectly honest, now that he had Lilibelle's confession, albeit secondhand, the relief of knowing that his grandfather was truly innocent nearly brought tears to his eyes.

He felt like jumping up and shouting and pumping his fists in the air. But, while the letter was a triumph for him, those few words were going to cut like a knife into the hearts of Con Delancey's family. So he restrained himself.

"Why are you doing this?" he asked. "You could have kept it, and there's no telling when I'd have been able to get the journal. Hell, I might have never gotten it."

"Why am I showing it to you?" she said, spreading

her hands. "Because it's the truth. Or at least the closest thing to the truth you'll get, outside of the journal."

He nodded. "But it's going to tear your family's hearts to pieces. You had no obligation to give me this."

That appeared to shock her. Her brow furrowed and she sent him an odd look. "We had a bargain," she said. "We agreed to find the truth."

That surprised him. He'd never expected her to share anything that would reflect badly upon her family.

"Jack?" Cara Lynn said. "What are you going to do?"

He didn't even hesitate. "I'm going to take this letter to the police and use it as probable cause to petition the court to run DNA on blood from the evidence file." He fanned the letter. "With any luck, this letter will be enough to convince the judge to reopen the case. And when he does, I believe the blood on the gun will turn out to be Lilibelle's."

"Blood?" Cara Lynn echoed. "What blood?"

"You've heard about the cases where wrongly convicted people are being freed because the court has allowed a review of DNA evidence in cases where the technology wasn't available when the case was originally tried?"

"Oh, well yes. I just didn't think about how old the evidence really was, I guess." She gazed at him thoughtfully for a moment. "From what I understand from listening to Harte talk about these things, isn't Aunt Claire's letter hearsay? I mean, her letter can't be entered into evidence, right?"

"It depends on the lawyer. I'm sure going to try to have it entered. We'll see what the judge says."

"But what about my grandmother's journal? If it says the same thing as Claire's letter, is that considered a confession? Will it be considered evidence in court?"

"I don't know. I'm playing this by ear. I'd like to think so, but I'm afraid it won't be. After all, even though the journal is handwritten and dated, and probably signed, I'm not sure it can be proven beyond the shadow of a doubt that it was your grandmother that wrote it, or that she was acting of her own free will when she did."

"So you have to get the approval for the DNA."

Jack nodded.

"Oh, my God. I have no idea what to tell my family." She looked at Jack. "How do I tell them?"

"Cara, there's no need to tell them at all. No need to worry or upset them until we have something conclusive."

"I don't know about that," she said. "I'm pretty sure this should be presented to Harte—he's the Delancey attorney."

Jack puffed his cheeks and blew out a breath in frustration. "I can guarantee you that within minutes of the petition's filing, your family will know."

"So you're not going to do anything? That seems sneaky."

He studied her for a few seconds. "If you feel that strongly, go ahead and tell them."

She looked back at him as doubt clouded her face. He knew exactly what she was thinking. She was weighing telling her family about Claire's revelation against her humiliation at being duped by Jacques Broussard. Then her brows drew down and her eyes narrowed.

"Jack, what if your grandfather's DNA is in the blood evidence?"

"It won't be."

"You don't know that. It was just Con and Grandmother and Armand Broussard up at the fishing cabin that day."

"That's not what my grandfather said."

"What do you mean?" Cara Lynn asked.

"Your cousin Paul was there," he said.

"Paul? Are you sure? I never heard that."

"Yes. It's what my grandfather said."

"But—he could have lied. I've never heard anyone talk about Paul. My grandmother didn't mention him in her letter and neither did Aunt Claire."

Jack stiffened. "He didn't lie."

"Come on, Jack. How do you know? You've never heard but one side of the story."

"He had no reason to lie."

"No reason? What about appeals? What about trying to get a new trial or parole?"

"Your family saw to it that his appeals failed and that someone was there at every parole hearing talking about the tragedy of Con Delancey's death and the grief of his poor widow."

"Sounds like you were there."

"I was. Ever since they finally let me in when I was eighteen." He stood and walked over to the refrigerator, opening it and staring at the contents. After a moment, he pulled out a bottle of sparkling water and opened it.

Cara Lynn wanted to tell him how sorry she was that he'd had to see his grandfather in prison orange. That he'd never had a father figure in his home with him and his mother, but she couldn't. He was angry.

Well, so was she. The two of them were like knights of old, jousting, using their own versions of the truth as weapons to dismount the other.

So instead, she took a deep breath to calm herself and asked what she thought was the next logical question. "But what if your grandfather's blood is on the weapon?"

He turned and stared at her, holding the bottle of water ready to turn and drink. After a brief, frowning silence, he answered. "Then, that's it. It'll be over."

"You'll be done with—us? With the Delanceys?"

"Yeah," he muttered, then lifted the cold bottle to his lips. Once he'd drunk his fill, he turned around, looking at the back of Cara Lynn's bowed head. She was looking at her hands. He had a feeling she was thinking about whatever was written on that second page of Claire's letter.

Ever since his misspent youth from which his Aunt Lilibelle had saved him, Paul had been fascinated with the police. He'd had a police scanner since the first Christmas he'd lived with her, and over the years he'd spent many hours listening to it.

Also, among his drinking buddies were a few friends from the old days. One of them was a dispatcher for the St. Tammany Parish Sheriff's Office. He kept Paul abreast of everything that went on in the county, especially having to do with the Delanceys, and in return, Paul picked up his bar tab.

So when the word got around that a petition had come in to reopen the Con Delancey murder case for comparison of DNA evidence, Paul found out within minutes. He went into a panic.

He'd done what any of the Delanceys would have done. He had protected his family, whatever the cost. But had his idea of protection gone outside the bounds of accepted behavior for law enforcement? And more importantly, for the Delanceys?

But right now, there was nothing he could do. He was going to have to wait and see what happened.

Cara Lynn had lied to him. There was a lot of interesting stuff in Jack Bush's briefcase—or to be accurate—Jacques Broussard's briefcase. But her letter from Lilibelle wasn't there. He should have been harsher. Maybe he should have hurt her or fired a shot into a pillow to scare her.

In a way, he admired her. She either had more courage or was more foolish than he'd given her credit for. While she'd known he'd have a hard time getting into the case, she hadn't had any idea how long it would take. She hadn't known that he would not come back and kill her as he'd promised. And now he needed that letter more than ever. It was obvious that Jack had used it to file a petition for DNA testing.

Paul was too nervous to sleep, too anxious and distracted to take his usual daily run. He spent day and night drinking coffee, often boosted with bourbon, and going through his receipts and invoices and bank statements of the past two decades, trying to cook his books so that it appeared that the majority of Claire Delancey's money that he'd spent had been on her house and not for his personal use. It was all he could manage to concentrate on as he waited for the journal and the letter's information to come out. As he waited for the police to come to arrest him.

TWO DAYS LATER, on Friday evening, Cara Lynn and Jack took her car to their mechanic for regular maintenance scheduled for the next day, then headed to Reilly and Christy's house, getting there at around six-thirty in the evening. Nicole, Ryker's wife, who was a professional chef, had prepared a spectacular array of light hors d'oeuvres, and made a mint-julep punch. Reilly had a full bar of wine and liquor, as well as iced tea and coffee.

Cara Lynn took a quick look around and saw that most of her brothers and cousins were there. Her cousin Hannah and her fiancé, Mack, were missing, because as soon as they had returned from France, they'd discovered that her mother's doctors were on alert that they might receive a liver within the next twenty-four hours. Then they'd heard of Claire's sudden death.

Cara Lynn's mom and dad had stayed home because her father had an infection and Betty was taking care of him.

"Reilly," she said, taking his hand and proffering her cheek for him to kiss. "And Christy. Congratulations! You look really good!" she said, bussing Christy's cheeks European style. "Although I've got to say that Reilly is the one glowing. I mean, look at that face."

She and Christy laughed while Reilly, cheeks red, endured some good-natured ribbing from his brothers and cousins.

In the crowd she saw Paul talking with Shel Rossi, a second cousin on the Delancey side who was a firefighter. Shel was with a striking woman she'd seen with him at the reception.

She looked at Paul, thinking about Armand Broussard's assertion that he was present when her grandmother shot Con Delancey. As she took Jack around and introduced him to the few people he hadn't already met, she tried to calculate Paul's age. She knew he'd been very young when his parents had been killed and he'd been taken in by her grandmother and grandfather. Lilibelle had always called him "her third son."

But Cara Lynn had no idea when he'd been born. Judging by his looks, he was likely in his mid to late forties.

So if he was forty-five today, then twenty-eight years ago when Con Delancey was murdered, he'd have been seventeen. A teenager. But why had Lilibelle not mentioned him in her letter—or for that matter, left him part of the Guillame estate, as she had her sons Robert and Michael? In fact, Cara Lynn had heard Paul talk all his life about his aunt's journals. She left Jack's side and approached Paul. He turned to her in greeting. "How is your research coming along?"

It amazed Cara Lynn that the world outside her apartment was apparently going on just as though nothing had happened. The family was aware of the theft of the journal and the tiara, of course, but nobody except Jack and her and the thief knew about the letters or Jack's true identity, or her attack.

"Cara Lynn?"

"Oh, Paul, sorry. I've had a headache for the past few days. I guess I'm zoning out a little. You're talking about the genealogy? I haven't done a thing with it since the last time you asked. I'm just so impossibly busy." She shrugged.

Paul smirked. "Ah, newlyweds," he said.

She raised her eyebrows. "Well—that's part of it."

"You know, Claire always told everyone they could store photos, tax records and other household papers too numerous to store in a safe deposit box on her third floor. She had a tin roof and heart-pine floors, nearly impermeable. Those rooms are as crowded as a spinster's attic. Boxes everywhere. But the one I've been talking about might be the biggest box of all. It's full of old letters, cards and old documents. I rifled through it, but it's crammed full. Some go back as far as the mid-eighteen hundreds."

"Wow," Cara Lynn said. "That might give me some insight into Con's mother's family. Her maiden name was Jones, but nobody seems to know what her mother's maiden name was. That makes it pretty difficult to get any further back on that side of the family. I'd love to have that box."

"I'll bring it over one day."

"Great," Cara Lynn said, smiling at him. "I can't wait to dig into it. Just give me a call."

"I'll do that." Paul gestured with his head for her to come closer. He put his left arm around her shoulders and reached for her right hand.

"Ow," she uttered. She lifted her hand and looked at her index finger. There was a tiny scratch on the inside of her knuckle. "Something scratched me."

"Oh," Paul said. "Sorry. It's this silver ring with the Austrian crystals. It catches on my clothes, too."

"It's okay," she said, touching her tongue to the scratch. "What were you saying?"

He was staring at her finger. "Hmm?"

She chuckled. "You seem as scatterbrained as I am. You were about to tell me something."

"Oh, right." He sent a glance around, then whispered to her. "I just want you to be careful. Every time I see your new husband, he looks as though he's casing the joint."

"Wha—?" Her chuckle turned into a nervous laugh. "Casing—? Paul, what are you implying? You make him sound like a jewel thief." Then, hearing her words, she recoiled. "Whoa! I hope you're not suggesting Jack may have hired that thief. That's ridiculous."

"I just know he was paying a lot more attention to where the thief was running than to his injured wife."

"Ryker and Ethan and Reilly did the same thing. They chased the guy instead of staying with me. They knew the others would check on me."

"Yeah, and also, they're cops. That's what they're trained to do. Jack's your husband." Paul gave her a sharp look. "Unless he is a cop?"

She shook her head. "Of course not. He's an architect."

Paul spread his hands and shrugged exaggeratedly just as Lucas walked up to them. "Paul," he said, nodding at the other man. Then he turned to Cara Lynn. "Hey, sugar. How's married life?"

She smiled. "Not bad. I'm hanging in there."

Lucas laughed. "I wanted to let you know that the guy we picked up after we ran the prints on the tiara may be about to break."

"Break?" Paul said. "You mean confess?"

"Not exactly. We've got him. His prints matched the partials on the tiara, which pretty much seals it, since we know the tiara had been sealed in that box until a couple of minutes prior to the lights going out. Plus he had the journal in his house."

"Right, right," Paul said.

"So what you want is who he's working for, right?" Cara Lynn said.

Lucas nodded. "Yeah."

"Of course," Paul said, waving a hand. "Cop Show 101. I forgot."

Cara Lynn chuckled. "I guess it's nice to know that the cop shows get some of it right."

"Hmph," was Lucas's only comment.

At that moment, Jack walked up with a glass of mint-julep punch for her.

"That looks good," Paul said. "I'm going to grab a glass, then I've got to go. Claire's lawyers are killing me. They want to see receipts for every dime I spent in the last twenty years. I'll be digging in boxes and bins all night long." With an absent nod in their direction, he hurried off.

Lucas watched Paul leave. "Claire's lawyers are on the right track, I'd say," he commented.

"Lucas," Cara Lynn admonished.

He shrugged. "He's lived the high life for all this time, with Aunt Claire footing the bill. If he's been on the up and up then he won't have a problem with the lawyers."

Cara Lynn took a sip of the punch and made a face. "I don't want this. I'm still queasy from that headache."

"Still?" Jack said. "I think your problem is you're a nervous wreck from everything that's happened."

She sent him an ironic look. "You think?"

Lucas kissed her on the forehead. "Bye, sugar. I need to go find the wife. I've got a long day tomorrow."

"We're going, too. I just need to go by and tell Reilly and Christy one more time how excited I am that they're pregnant." Cara Lynn was glad to be going home. She was exhausted, and there was still something nagging at her brain. Something she should remember about the man who attacked her, but couldn't.

Chapter Eleven

Cara Lynn slept late the next morning. When she woke, the sun was shining in the bedroom window. She automatically squinted, then realized that squinting wasn't necessary. The headache that had been lingering ever since the reception over a week before had finally disappeared.

She smelled coffee, but when she went into the living room, Jack wasn't there. He'd folded the sheet and blanket he'd used and stacked them on the end of the couch.

He hadn't mentioned what he planned to do today, but it wasn't hard to guess. If he had a lawyer, and she was pretty sure he did, then they were probably looking for a judge sympathetic to Jack's grandfather's story.

Cara Lynn considered the question she'd asked herself time and time again since finding out Jack's true identity. What would it do to her family if a judge agreed to reopen the Con Delancey murder case?

"I guess we're about to find out," she muttered.

Cara Lynn looked around. There were newspapers and unopened mail strewn on the coffee table. Jack had rinsed the dishes, but hadn't put them in the dishwasher. She needed to wash clothes. The hamper was full.

Today was definitely a day to spend at home, since her car was in the shop. She'd clean up, wash and fold some clothes and just generally take it easy. She might get to finish reading that novel she'd started a few weeks ago. And if she still felt good later, she could fix another nice dinner for Jack. She smiled, thinking about puttering around in the kitchen like a housewife.

But the word housewife echoed in her head like a ghostly wail in a haunted house. She wasn't a housewife. She wasn't a wife at all. Not really. Her marriage was a sham. Her husband wasn't even who he said he was. She had no doubt that as soon as he was able to clear his grandfather's name, he'd be gone and she'd be left alone and humiliated. Suddenly, puttering about her apartment and waiting for Jack to get back from a meeting with his lawyer was starting to sound sad and pathetic.

She set her coffee cup down half full and headed to the bathroom. She'd shower and wash her hair. Then she'd see what she really wanted to do today. There was plenty to choose from. She had a new piece she was working on at her studio, and last night at Reilly and Christy's, Kate had asked her if she wanted to go to lunch one day. Maybe Kate would want to do that today.

She got into the shower and turned on the hot water so it cascaded over her head and body. The steam felt wonderful. She felt as though she could stay there, letting the hot water sluice tension, heartache and exhaustion down the drain. If she could manipulate time as

easily as she could the shower knobs, she'd turn it back
to the day she met Jack.

By skipping the rest of her show to go with him that
night, she'd set all this in motion. If she could go back,
she would refuse his outrageous request. Would he have
kept trying, she wondered? In thinking about the answer
to that, which was yes, she accepted the truth, which
was that no matter what the outcome of all this was, no
matter if she were left alone and heartbroken, she was
glad she'd known Jack Bush.

She wouldn't have missed it for the world.

Her throat tightened and her eyes stung as she poured
some shampoo and started washing her hair. The soap
stung the right side of her neck, just at the curve of
her shoulder, and she remembered Jack telling her she
had tiny scratches there. She touched the place that
burned. Her fingers were slick with water and soap
but she could still feel a patch of tiny scabs where the
scratches had been. She couldn't remember how she'd
gotten it. Maybe she'd left a cardboard tag or a pin in
a dress.

She quickly finished, dried off and wrapped a towel
around her head, turban-style, and slipped her arms into
a terry cloth bathrobe, then walked into the kitchen to
get her half-drunk coffee.

While she was topping off her cup, she heard a noise
that sounded like it was coming from her office. "Jack?"
she called, walking down the hall. "Jack, is that you?"

But it wasn't Jack who appeared at the office door.

"Paul!" she cried. Her hand jerked and coffee spilled
over the side of the cup. Luckily it wasn't too hot. She

covered her pounding heart with her other hand. "Oh, my God. Wh—what are you doing here? You nearly scared the life out of me."

Paul smiled at her.

"How did you get in?" She glanced in the direction of the living room. "Did Jack leave the door unlocked?" She knew better. Jack wouldn't do that.

Paul still didn't speak.

Cara Lynn didn't like the look on his face. He was still smiling, but it wasn't a nice smile. And it didn't go with his dark eyes, which were too hard, like a brittle piece of black glass that would shatter at the slightest blow.

She caught the lapels of the terry cloth robe and pulled them together at her neck. "What's going on, Paul? How did you get in here?"

He stepped toward her and she recoiled automatically, but he merely passed her and walked up the hall toward the kitchen. She followed him.

"Remember I told you about the big box of legal documents and letters dating back to the eighteen fifties? I thought I'd bring it over for you this morning. If you want to, we can go through some of it together. It's really interesting." He gestured back toward the office. "I set it in your office so you wouldn't have to carry it," he finished amiably, as if they'd planned to do this today.

Cara clutched the lapels of the robe more tightly. With every second that went by she was more convinced that there was something very wrong about Paul showing up like this. She didn't for one second believe he had come out to Chef Voleur at this time of the day just to bring her a box and talk about genealogy.

But what bothered her most was that he had *broken* into her home. He had never had a key and there wasn't one hidden outside.

"Paul, how did you get in?" she asked again.

Paul smiled at her. "Oh, I have a few tricks up my sleeve from my delinquent youth," he said. "I didn't mean to scare you. I just tell my friends to come on into the house if I don't hear the doorbell. And you know, time was that none of us locked our houses." He walked over to the living room window and looked out. "It really looked like rain earlier, but now I see the sun's out. That's good. I thought I'd go out and take some photos of gravestones this afternoon. I'm so tired of digging through boxes and sorting receipts for those damn lawyers. I'd much rather be helping you with the genealogy. Do you want to come with?"

Those words, coming from cynical, sarcastic Paul sounded ludicrous. He wasn't a *come with* kind of guy. In fact, he wasn't a *taking photographs on a nice afternoon* kind of guy, either. No. Paul disliked the sun. According to family members who knew him better than she did, he did most of his renovation work on Claire's house at night.

"I told you last night that I don't have time to work on the genealogy. I'm much too busy right now." Then she gestured toward her towel-wrapped hair and her terry cloth robe. "Thanks for the box, but I need you to go now." Her uneasiness was fast moving toward fear. This was probably the longest she'd ever talked to

Paul, and with every second that passed, he was acting weirder and creepier.

"I didn't mean to scare you, sweetie. I'm sorry. I was just trying to help."

She thought about the missing bottles of water. "Have you been in my apartment before when we weren't here?"

He looked affronted. "Of course not. Why would I?" He gestured toward the office. "I only just brought that box of papers down from Claire's attic." He put the smile on again, but it still wasn't real.

"Okay," he said on a sigh. "I'm going to go now. I do apologize. I should have kept my little lock-picking secrets to myself. I certainly didn't mean any harm." He gave her a hangdog look and headed for the door.

Cara Lynn was torn between *good riddance* and being politely grateful for the box, which really would, admittedly, make her job a lot easier.

But as soon as Jack got home, she was going to demand that he go out and get the best double-locking deadbolt they made—or whatever kind of lock would completely protect them from Paul's *lock-picking* skills.

"Oh, by the way," Paul said, turning at the door. "Where's Jack?"

Cara Lynn shook her head. "He left early. He had some business—in Biloxi, I think." The lie came quickly and easily to her lips. They hadn't talked to anyone in the family—except Ryker—about Jack's efforts to have the DNA examined. So she didn't want to tell Paul, who was known to be a huge gossip.

Paul nodded. His gaze shifted from her to the couch, then back to her again. "Trouble in paradise?" he asked.

"What?" She followed his gaze. "Oh, no." She held up a hand to ward off any misconception, hoping he wouldn't spread the word about Jack sleeping on the couch. "No. He's been working late on some architectural design he's doing for a casino company."

"Damn things are ruining the coastline."

Cara Lynn shrugged. "I suppose so." She stood there, waiting for him to leave. She watched him. He had a permanent slump, the type some very slender men get as they grow older. His hair was that ridiculous black that had never existed in nature, and she saw that the elbows of his sport coat were worn. Was that neglect or lack of money? She'd always heard that he lived off Claire's money while he kept her house in a perpetual state of renovation. Maybe he didn't live the high life as much as everyone thought he did.

"Call me if you decide you want to go look at gravestones," he said, disappointment obvious in his voice, as he reached for the doorknob.

Despite her uneasy feeling, despite her irritation at him for picking the lock and walking into her apartment, her natural kindness and graciousness took the place of her good sense.

"Paul, would you like some coffee?" she asked. As soon as the words left her lips she regretted them. She didn't want him here. She'd never really liked him.

Paul turned, his arms thrown out for a hug or a grand gesture, she supposed. His right hand hit hers and something scratched her wrist.

"Ow!" she cried, recoiling. She looked at her wrist and saw a thin scratch across the inside of it. It hardly raised a drop of blood but it stung. Like her knuckle, she thought, remembering when his Austrian crystal ring had scratched her at Reilly and Christy's party.

That sense of something important hovering just outside the reach of her conscious mind came over her again and she swayed, vision going dark and sparkly for an instant.

"Cara Lynn? What's wrong?" Paul asked in a solicitous voice.

She shook her head to clear it. "Oh, nothing, really. I've had this headache clinging on for days. I thought it was gone this morning, but now it's starting back up again. I probably should call my doctor and get him to prescribe me something for it."

Paul was watching her closely. "I'm sure those headaches can be a bitch," he said. "I'm sorry."

For a brief moment, Cara Lynn thought he might finally leave, thinking she needed to lie down because of her headache. She put her hand to her temple, hoping he'd take the hint.

Instead, he released the doorknob and said, "Why don't you change clothes and I'll pull out some of the more interesting documents from the box."

"Paul, I told you I'm too busy."

He gave no indication that he'd heard her and instead headed toward her kitchen.

Cara faced the choice of spending the morning in a wet robe and towel or changing. She wished for a third choice—Paul leaving, but apparently that wasn't going to happen, at least not any time soon.

She wasn't comfortable leaving Paul in the kitchen alone. But she went into the bedroom and changed in record time. Grabbing a comb, she hurried back into the kitchen.

Paul was still at the table. He had a selection of items—her items, from her hiding place behind the baseboard, spread out around him and was fingering them with his right hand. Each time he moved his hand, light glanced off the ring he wore.

Cara stared—not at the items, but at the ring. When she did, a flash of memory slammed her. She remembered the man's hand pushing the barrel of the gun into her flesh, remembered its weight on the side of her neck and now, thinking about it, she remembered the tiny scratching sensations that she hadn't noticed at the time because of her fear. She touched the scratch on her knuckle and the new one on her wrist.

"Paul—" she gasped. "You? That was you?" she whispered, stepping backward, away from him. "You attacked me. You put a gun to my neck. That ring scratched me. Oh, my God—and how—how did you find my hiding place?" she cried. Now, she was afraid. He'd come into her house. He'd attacked her. He'd found her hiding place and gone through her purse. What else had he done? What else was he capable of doing?

"I'm taking some of the things that should have been mine," he said calmly. "Or at least some substitute for what my Aunt Lili always promised me."

"You need to leave," she said. "Now. Or I'm calling Ryker."

He shook his head. "Do you know how long it took me to find your secret hiding place? Well, it took a long time."

"You have been in here. You drank our water."

He shook his head. "Cara Lynn, why did you hook up with Broussard? Did he really seduce you? Were you that easily duped?"

"You know? You know who he is?"

"Of course. I've known from the beginning. Well, almost the beginning. I mean really—Bush? Broussard? That's amateur. I could have come up with something a lot better. Hell—*you* could have."

Cara Lynn stared at her cousin, trying to figure out exactly what he wanted. His ironic voice had turned as hard and brittle as his eyes. A nauseating dread hit the pit of her stomach. "What do you want? I don't care. Take anything you want. I'm not that into the great big flashy stuff. You want the emeralds? Be my guest."

"What I want is Aunt Lili's last journal and your grandmother's letter. Claire's letter, which I found tucked into your purse, thank you very much, is not enough by itself. I need the one that was handwritten by Aunt Lili."

"Why?" she asked, trying to understand. Then she remembered what Jack had told her. "You were there at the fishing cabin when Con was killed." She looked at him. "Did you kill my grandfather? And how did you manage to get Lili to cover up the fact that you were there? The police didn't even know you were there. Nobody did, except Jack's grandfather." She stopped.

He shrugged. "I told you I needed that letter." Paul reached down into the pocket of his jacket and pulled out a fairly large, shiny handgun. "And you lied to me. You said it was in the briefcase." He held the gun up, pointed at her.

"Where is Aunt Lili's letter, Cara Lynn?"

Chapter Twelve

"Obviously, we won't be able to file the petition until Monday," Jasper Barkley said, leaning back in his executive chair. "But we've got a sympathetic judge. It doesn't hurt that his son was accused of assault and was exonerated by DNA evidence. He believes in it and your grandfather's story touched him."

"It doesn't hurt that his father lost a local representative seat to Con Delancey back in the day, either," Greg Haymore said.

Jack was amazed at his luck. Actually, he was amazed at Haymore's connections. When he'd told him he had Con Delancey's wife's letter, in which she confessed to killing the infamous politician, Haymore immediately contacted Jasper Barkley, whom he called *the best-connected attorney in the state*. He'd reported back to Jack within an hour that Barkley had started researching which judges would most likely be sympathetic to Jack's efforts to clear his grandfather's name.

Barkley had found Judge Morris VanDerBridge, Jr., the son of Representative Morrison VanDerBridge, Sr., who had been a bitter rival of Con Delancey during their entire careers.

He and Haymore stood and said goodbye to Jasper Barkley, and talked as they walked back to their cars.

"I can't believe you did it," Jack said. "This judge VanDerBridge is perfect."

Haymore lit a cigarette. "It's not like there's a shortage of people around here who weren't fans of Con Delancey."

"Yeah, but there's no shortage of people who loved him, either."

Haymore pointed toward Jack with his cigarette. "But most of the ones who *didn't* like him are in politics or law, and that's what you needed." He stopped at a street crossing. "Hey, why don't you let me buy you a drink?"

Jack shook his head. "No. I need to get home. I'm not sure how Cara Lynn is going to react to the news, but I need to get home and let her know. I don't like leaving her alone, either. She's been nervous ever since that guy broke in."

"Yeah, you should have let me come in and go over the place. I might have been able to find something. I can take fingerprints and I have a way of getting them run, if I don't use it too often. But that's fine. I tell you what. We'll get that drink later—after we clear your granddad's name."

"Count on it," Jack said and shook Haymore's hand. "I guess Barkley will call you?"

Haymore nodded. "I'll let you know as soon as I hear from him. We'll need to arrange for you and him to meet with Judge VanDerBridge. He can sign the petition to reopen the case and then you'll be on your way." The light turned and Haymore headed across the street.

"Thanks again," Jack called as he reached his car and got in. When he got on to the Pontchartrain Causeway to head back to Chef Voleur, he pressed the call button on his car's steering wheel, activating the Bluetooth.

"Dial name," he said.

When the computer asked him what name, he said, "Cara Lynn."

The computer dialed and her cell phone rang until it went to voice mail. A glance at the dashboard told him it was almost noon. She wouldn't still be in bed. So where was she? He supposed she could be in the shower or out with a friend. Since her car was in the shop, she'd said she was looking forward to a quiet day at home.

She'd also mentioned washing clothes and that damned washing machine was loud. She might not be able to hear her phone.

He sighed and hung up. It would be better to tell her to her face about his success in finding a judge who would retry the case allowing DNA evidence. It occurred to him that deep down, he believed—or wanted to believe—that she'd be as excited about the retrial as he was.

How did he keep forgetting that to her, he was the enemy? He was the man who was going to change everything the Delancey family had ever believed about their beloved grandmother.

When he was halfway across the causeway, he called her cell phone again, and again it went to voice mail. He didn't like that. Not one bit. She almost always answered her cell. And there was a man out there somewhere who had gotten into their apartment and attacked her. Who had held a gun at her throat and threatened her life.

"Come on, Cara, go find your phone. Check your messages."

Looking at the line of traffic, he figured it was going to be at least another half hour before he was off the causeway and headed for Chef Voleur.

He debated calling one of her brothers or cousins to check on her. If she was at home and fine, she would be furious and whoever he called would be suspicious about why Jack was so concerned that he hadn't been able to reach Cara Lynn for a couple of hours.

Ahead of him, brake lights flashed one after the other like dominos falling along the straight length of the Pontchartrain Causeway. With a muttered growl, Jack pressed the call button again.

When the computer asked what name, he said, "Detective Ryker Delancey."

CARA LYNN LISTENED as the last echo of her ringing phone faded. She couldn't take her eyes off it. *Please know there's something wrong.*

"Is that your special ring for Jack?" Paul asked. "It's very sweet."

"What are you planning? Are we just going to sit here until Jack comes home?"

"We're going to sit here until you tell me where that letter is."

"I've told you, I don't know," Cara Lynn said. "I can't just produce it out of thin air."

Paul brandished the gun. "Don't get smart with me, girl. I'm twenty years older than you are. You need to pay me the respect I deserve."

"You're sitting there with a gun held on a member of your family, Paul. How much respect does that deserve?"

"If you don't watch out, I'm going to backhand you across your smart mouth with this ring. We'll see how many scratches that'll make."

She hardly recognized Paul now. He'd always seemed so mild. A little effeminate, a little fey, but never ever violent. She'd liked him when she was younger, because he was the most interesting person to sit next to at a family get-together. He had a hilarious comment about almost everything and everyone. Most of them were not very complimentary, but all of them were true, either in whole or in part. Once she'd asked him what kind of comments he made about her when she wasn't around.

He'd looked at her somberly and said, *Honey, who would I talk to about you? You're their little princess. I'd have to pick up homeless men off the street to find someone who didn't know you and wouldn't take offense if I said one derogatory word about you.*

At the time she'd liked being called a princess. Now though, thinking back, she realized what a bitter monologue he'd delivered in answer to her innocent twelve-year-old's question.

"Do you hate me, Paul?"

"Where's that coming from?" he asked, chuckling a little.

"I was just thinking about the day I asked you what you said about me when you were talking to other people. Your answer was kind of mean."

"Was it? Well, sweetie, I don't know if I'd say *hate*. That's such a strong word. I resent you. I'm jealous of you. I envy you, but then I envy all the Delancey grandkids. I don't know how you managed to charm Lilibelle into giving you everything. But then, I've always been the bastard son. Lili took me in when I was on my way to Juvie. She saved me." He paused and rubbed at the corner of one eye. "I loved her," he said sternly. "Do you understand what I'm saying?"

Cara Lynn opened her mouth, but before she could draw breath to speak, Paul shouted at her. "Do you?"

"Of—of course," she stammered. "She took you in. In effect, she was your mother."

"No!" He slammed a palm down on the table. "I *loved* her."

Cara swallowed. "Oh," she murmured, then, "What now? What do you want? You've got Claire's letter. You've got the emerald necklace, my cash. What now?"

"I have to have Lili's letter! How dense are you? That's all I've been talking about. That and her journal."

"I don't know where it is. I thought it was in the briefcase."

"I know that's a lie. You knew it wasn't in the case. You thought you were being so clever. You're lucky I didn't come back and kill you."

She had to agree with him on that. "You wouldn't

hurt me," she said to Paul. Even to herself the statement sounded more like a question. But as she said it,
she began to understand. Everything was beginning
to coalesce into one whole. They were no longer a pile
of separate, jagged pieces that didn't make any sense.

"How the hell do you know what I would or wouldn't
do?"

She smiled sadly. "You couldn't kill me. I do know,
because you couldn't kill my grandfather, either, could
you?"

Paul's face went white as a sheet and tiny drops of
sweat popped out on his forehead and his upper lip.
"Y-you have no idea wh-what you're talking about," he
stuttered as he wiped his face. "No idea."

"Yes, I do. You told Lili you'd kill Con for her,
didn't you? But then you couldn't." She saw on his pale,
pinched face that she was right. "You don't want Lili's
letter and her last journal to protect yourself. You want
it to protect *her*."

Paul switched the handgun from his right to his left
hand and flexed his cramped fingers. "You need to shut
up," he said. "Or you'll find out just what I *can* do."

"Lili took the gun and shot Con when you couldn't.
She shot him to protect you and you've done all this to
protect her."

JACK PARKED AT Cara Lynn's apartment and got out of
his car. A white BMW pulled in next to him and Detective Ryker Delancey got out, talking on his cell phone.

"Right," Ryker said. "The next street. Position the ve-
hicles behind the apartment building. I don't want him

to be able to see the police cars. No sirens. No lights. Got that? Good. Out." He flipped his phone closed and walked up to Jack. "You were right," he said, pointing to a shiny dark green Mercedes that was at least twenty years old. "That's Paul's car."

"I knew it. Can we hurry up? I don't like all this delay."

"I called the uniformed patrol officers as soon as I recognized Paul's car. They'll be here within a couple of minutes. They're parking behind the apartment. That'll give us just enough time to get you hooked up."

"Hooked up? To what?"

"I'm sending you in there, as if you're just getting home. Paul has become more and more desperate," Ryker said. "And we know Cara Lynn is in there."

"You know for sure?"

Ryker looked down at his feet. "We've got a camera in there."

Jack wasn't sure he heard right. "What? A camera? In where? In there?" His scalp tightened and his face grew hot. "What the hell? You've been spying on us? That's disgusting. Where?"

"Where's the camera? It's beside the front door, mounted on the curtain rod. It points toward the kitchen."

"No camera in—in the bedroom?" he asked through clenched teeth.

Ryker sent Jack an odd look. "No," he said, then after a moment he continued. "So she's in there and Paul is holding a gun on her. So I've got to treat this as a hostage situation. We'll be in place out here—"

"So you're sending *only me* in?"

Ryker nodded. "I know this is not standard procedure by any means, but Cara Lynn will trust you and Paul won't feel threatened by you like he will with any of us. I know you can do this. Just go in as though you have no idea there's anything wrong. Once you're inside, my best guess is you'll become a hostage, too."

"Not if I can help it," Jack said.

Ryker put a hand on Jack's shoulder. "Listen to me," he said. "I understand how you feel. But my only other choice is to send in SWAT." He squeezed Jack's shoulder. "And I *really* don't want to do that. I believe you can do this. Can I count on you?"

Jack clenched his teeth. "Of course," he said.

Ryker gave his shoulder one more squeeze, then let go. His cell phone chirped and he answered it. "Yeah? Right. Bring the van around here to the parking lot. Everybody else in place?"

An innocuous van pulled into the parking lot behind Ryker's BMW. Its side panel door opened. "Come on, Jack, let's go."

Jack frowned. "What's this?"

"For one thing, it's where the lab tech is going to get you hooked up to our monitors. I'll show you what else when we get inside."

Jack got into the van behind Ryker. The inside of the vehicle looked like a setup at NASA or something. There was a laptop, several tablets, a small screen mounted on the side of the van, and microphones, small but obviously powerful speakers, black boxes, other instruments Jack couldn't identify, and a huge tangle of wires everywhere.

"What the hell?" he muttered.

"It's a surveillance van," Ryker started.

"That much I got. Am I going to have a camera as well as a microphone?"

Ryker shook his head as his eyes searched Jack's face. "Is there anything we ought to know before we go in, Jack?"

For some reason, the question, asked in Ryker's quiet, controlled voice, made Jack feel as though an anvil the size of the van had lifted off his chest. He blew out a breath and nodded.

"My name is not actually Jack Bush," he said, looking at his hands and not at Ryker. "I was christened Jacques. Jacques Broussard. I'm—"

"Armand Broussard's grandson," Ryker finished. "I know."

"You know?" Jack said, surprised. So Cara *had* gone to her family. He felt disappointed, although he knew that wasn't fair to her. He'd put her in an impossible situation. He should have realized that he could be placing her in danger with his ridiculous game.

"Jack," Ryker said.

Jack realized it was the second time the detective had called his name in the past few seconds. He looked up at him.

"Cara Lynn didn't tell me," Ryker said. "And we haven't mentioned anything to her. But I've got to tell you, Lucas and I have been looking into your background ever since we first knew anything about you."

Jack began to process that information. The Delanceys knew who he was and they hadn't rushed him, beat him up, thrown him out or put him in jail. Nor had they jerked Cara Lynn away from him for her protection. But they had been spying on him—on them—for who knew how long. Probably the whole time. He felt his jaw clench again.

"Okay, then. Let's get started. You're going to be wearing a watch that's actually a smartphone. Your biggest problem is going to be to pretend it's just a watch. There's a tendency to play with it, which distorts the sound. Also, a lot of people can't keep their eyes off it or tend to hold it up, thinking either consciously or subconsciously that aiming it is going to help sound quality. You can't do any of that." He handed the watch to Jack. "Put it on in place of your watch and then forget it."

Jack took the watch and put it on his left wrist, studied it for a couple of seconds, then nodded. After a slight pause, he looked up at Ryker. "Can I ask you something about your—surveillance?"

Ryker sent him a sidelong look. "Save it. We're ready to go."

RYKER SAT DOWN next to the tech and asked, "What have you heard so far?" as he focused on the screen before him. What he saw made him want to tear out of the van, break down the apartment door with his gun out and ready to shoot Paul Guillame.

Paul and Cara Lynn were sitting at the kitchen table. Paul held a handgun on her and she had her hands clasped in front of her on the table. Erase the gun from the picture and it looked as though they were having a pleasant conversation, although Ryker couldn't hear anything and wouldn't be able to until Jack got inside with the watch-phone.

Ryker rubbed a hand over his face and opened his cell phone and pressed a button. "In place?" he asked.

"Yes, sir," Reilly Delancey replied. "I'm in position. I've got the solution, if necessary."

Ryker nodded to himself. His twin brother, Reilly, was one of the best snipers in the state, maybe the nation. If he said he had the solution, then he had a straight shot, and if Ryker gave the word, Paul Guillame would be dead. "Hold steady, Reilly," he said. "Out."

"WHAT DO YOU think you're going to do when Jack walks in that door?" Cara Lynn asked Paul.

Paul lifted his gun hand and cradled it in his left hand, which he propped on the kitchen table.

"Your hand must be getting tired."

"I can hold out as long as you can, sweetie. Longer."

"You can't win against Jack. He's almost twenty years younger than you, and a lot stronger."

"I don't have to win against him physically. I just have to outsmart him, and I know his weakness."

Cara Lynn looked at her cousin, who was smirking at her. "What weakness?"

"Don't underestimate me. I know people. I watch them. I understand them. I've watched your husband. He won't let anything happen to you. He loves you too much."

She shook her head. "You're wrong about that. The bedclothes over there?" she nodded toward the couch. "You were right the first time. We aren't sleeping together. Haven't been for quite some time. You know who he is. He married me for one reason and one reason only. To clear his grandfather's name. To do that, he'll destroy my grandmother—my whole family— even me. I refused to help him. In fact, that's what he's doing today. He's talking to a private detective, trying to figure out a way to get the police to let him get a look at that last journal."

Paul assessed her, his brow furrowing into a frown. "I don't think I believe you. I'd like to. I'd like to think you feel the same way I do, even if it's not for the same reason. I could use your help in protecting Lili's name. But you're not that kind. You're an idealist, just like your husband. You believe that in the end, truth and justice are what's important. So if you believe that Lili was guilty, you'll be on Jack's side. Not to mention that you're totally in love with him."

"No, you're wrong."

"About what? Being on Jack's side or being in love with him. I'm not wrong. Come on. You've read the old man's letters, just like I have. I've read everything Jack had in that briefcase. Armand Broussard told the truth, as he saw it. He wrote down the facts. But I am the only person alive now who knows and understands the truth."

"Paul, I believe you. I'm not—"

"Oh, shut up, little princess. Do you know why Lilibelle wanted Con dead? Because he wouldn't leave that whore Kit Powers. He wanted to be governor and he was so arrogant that he thought he could win and the people of Louisiana would let him bring her into the governor's mansion while poor Aunt Lili lived alone, humiliated by her cheating husband."

Cara Lynn saw the anguish in Paul's eyes and remembered what he'd told her. He'd loved his aunt—been in love with her. "And what about you? Why did you want Con dead?"

When he answered, he wasn't looking at her. He was looking into the past. "She loved Con. He was her whole life. Every time he was unfaithful to her, he destroyed another part of her heart. But none of his whores hurt her like Kit Powers did. Do you know why?" He didn't wait for her to answer. Cara Lynn wasn't even sure that he remembered that she was there. "Because Con loved Kit. He never appreciated Lili's background and breeding. He killed her. She was alive but her heart was dead." Paul sighed and looked down at the gun in his hand.

He frowned, then looked up at Cara, and she knew he'd forgotten she was there until this moment. If she had been more clever, she probably could have taken the gun from his hand while he was lost in the past.

"I wanted him dead for two reasons, little princess. Because I loved Lili and because he didn't."

"I'm sorry for you, Paul. I'm sorry that Lili didn't love you. I'm sorry you spent your whole life longing for something you could never have. It's sad."

"Shut up! What do you know about love? You couldn't even see through Broussard's pathetically transparent deceit."

Cara Lynn was tired. Her jaw and her back ached from tension. She longed for the sound of Jack's key in the door, but at the same time she was terrified that when he walked in, Paul would shoot him. The war inside her, between wanting Jack to save her and wanting to keep him safe was ripping her in two.

At that instant, the sound of a key being inserted and turned in a lock screeched unnaturally in the silence of the apartment.

Cara Lynn froze. "Jack," she whispered.

WHEN JACK UNLOCKED the front door, he wondered if the image he'd seen on the surveillance van's screen was what he would see. His key sounding in the lock could spur Paul to sudden, violent action. The sight of the weapon in Paul's hand pointed at Cara Lynn had made Jack afraid that by walking into the apartment, he was putting Cara Lynn in more danger.

What if Paul was surprised by his sudden entrance? What if he panicked and shot Cara Lynn? Jack knew he wouldn't be able to stand it if anything happened to her. If Paul shot her because of him, he had no idea if he could even remain sane.

He pushed the door open, expecting to see Paul sitting and pointing a handgun at Cara Lynn. Even so, the sight took his breath away.

She was sitting at the kitchen table, her back stiff,

her hands clasped in front of her. Her hair cascaded in fat ringlets down past her neck, the way he liked it. The way it looked when she let it dry naturally.

Sitting facing Jack, his right hand holding a handgun pointed straight at Cara Lynn's heart was Paul.

Chapter Thirteen

"Hold it right there, Bush—Broussard. Or I'll put a bullet in Cara Lynn, right here, right now. Put your hands out—way out."

Jack complied and held his hands out at an angle from his body, so that Paul could see them. Ryker was right about the watch-phone. It was almost impossible to ignore it. Although he always wore a watch, he was so acutely conscious of the specially designed device on his wrist that it was all he could do not to twist his neck and look at it.

"Turn around—all the way around, and keep those hands out."

Jack stood there, looking at Paul.

"Do it!" Paul snapped.

Jack did it. "What are you doing, Paul? What do you plan to do, now that you've got us? Because I can tell you right now if you come near me you'll regret it. And if you try anything with Cara, I'll kill you with my bare hands."

"Shut up! Shut! Up!" Paul screamed. "Don't say another word. I know exactly what I'm doing. Tell him, Cara Lynn."

Jack looked directly at Cara Lynn for the first time.

Her eyes were wide, with pale blue shadows beneath them. "He knows what he's doing, Ja—"

Her voice broke on his name. He wanted to go to her, but he knew better.

"Empty your pockets," Paul said.

"What? Why?" Jack asked.

"Don't talk back to me, you punk. Just do what I say."

Jack shrugged, then started to reach into his right pocket.

"Hold it!" Paul cried. "Put your right hand on your head. Use your left hand to empty your right pocket."

Jack chuckled wryly. "I don't know, Paul. That sounds complicated."

"I'm warning you, Bush!"

Awkwardly, Jack reached into his right pants pocket with his left hand and dug out change, a disposable cigarette lighter, and a torn slip of paper. One by one, he set each item on the foyer table.

"Now the other pocket. Left on your head. Right hand in your pocket."

Jack did as he was told. "My wallet's in my back pocket, Paul," he said. "How do you want me to get it out?"

"You keep mouthing off to me and I'll make you sorry you did. Lift your right pants leg with your left hand. I want to make sure you don't have a weapon in there."

"Paul, you've lived around the Delanceys too long. I'm not a cop. I'm not an investigator. I'm just an architect."

"Stop talking and just do what I say."

Jack shrugged and obeyed him.

"The other leg. Right hand."

Jack lifted his left pant leg. "All done. Now what?" he asked. "I'm still trying to figure out what you're planning to do."

"Tell him, Cara Lynn."

Cara Lynn looked from Paul to Jack and back to Paul. She looked terrified. Jack wanted to send her a reassuring smile, but he didn't know how Paul would react.

"He's going to Paris," she said softly.

"Paris," Jack said, as if considering it. He knew that if he could get close enough to Paul he could overpower him, but the gun was an unknown. Or maybe he should say that *Paul* holding a gun was an unknown.

If he rushed him, would he panic and freeze, or panic and shoot? Jack was pretty sure the *panic* part was correct. It appeared by the way he constantly looked down at the weapon and flexed his fingers, plus the way that sweat was forming and dribbling down his temples and his neck, that he was not used to holding a gun. That made him very dangerous.

Paul moved and Jack tensed. But apparently all Paul was doing was fishing something out of his back pocket. Flexible plastic ties.

"I'm going to give Cara Lynn these two flex cuffs," Paul said. "But first, take off that watch."

"My watch?" Jack said, worried that Paul might decide to examine it. If he did, he just might figure out that it was a phone. Jack quickly unbuckled the band and took the watch off. He bent and set it on the floor.

"Now get your hands behind your back and walk over to that wall and stick your nose against it. She'll cuff you. Then, once you're incapacitated, I'll cuff her."

"Come on, man, you know you're not going to get anywhere. I mean, *Paris? Really?* You won't make it out of the city."

Paul stood and walked over behind Cara Lynn. He put his left hand on her shoulder and stuck the gun's barrel to her temple. "Do it."

Jack's scalp burned with anger and his pulse pounded with fear, but he did what Paul told him to. Once his nose was against the wall, he held his hands together behind him, fists crossed.

He wished there was a way to communicate with Cara Lynn to leave the ties loose, so he could easily break one. He'd never done it but he'd seen it done—on a TV show. It had looked easy, but it had also looked as though the flex cuffs were breakaways. Still, it was the only example he had of someone breaking out of them, so he hoped to hell it would work. The real question was going to be whether he could get them off or break them before Paul figured out what he was doing.

Once Jack was in position, Paul ordered Cara Lynn to stand. "Here. Take these. They're like regular plastic ties," he told her. "When you insert the end into the latch, you can only pull it one way—tighter. So wrap the first one around one wrist and pull it tight. Then take the second one and loop it through the first one, then wrap it around his other wrist the same way. Attach it so that the two ties are looped together and *tight*. Got it?

"Jack, Cara is going to come up behind you and I'm going to be right by her side. You try anything and I *will* shoot her. Do you believe me?"

Jack silently swore to kill Paul if he could get his hands on him. He nodded. He heard them approaching.

"Stand still, Jack, or you know what'll happen."

Jack held his arms rigid and his hands just far enough apart that Cara Lynn couldn't pull the second cuff completely tight against his resistance. She tried a couple of times to tighten it then finally gave up.

Jack felt pretty sure that everything Paul knew about flex cuffs he'd learned from an ad in a magazine or from the internet. He doubted seriously that Paul had ever actually cuffed anyone. Still, he held his breath as Paul gave Cara Lynn's handiwork a cursory examination.

"Now, back away, Cara Lynn. That's right. Two more steps. Jack, on the floor. On your stomach."

Cara Lynn watched Paul ordering her husband around with growing fear. She'd never seen Paul like this. He seemed not only angry, but excited. His gun hand was trembling slightly and his voice was tight with tension. She watched him closely, wondering if there was a way she could sneak up on him when he was so engrossed in making sure Jack was effectively trussed, that he'd forgotten about her.

"What the hell do you think you're doing, Paul?" Jack said, starting to taunt him again.

Cara wanted to yell at him to shut up, that he couldn't see Paul's face like she could. Paul appeared to almost be at his breaking point. She wasn't sure how much longer he could last. The trembling in his gun hand had spread to his other hand, his arms and shoulders, and she could even see his lips quivering.

Jack kept talking. "Do you think you're in some movie you're directing in your head? Holding us at gunpoint. Cuffing me hand and foot. Flying off to Paris. You're deluded. Don't you know that the Delanceys are onto you?"

"Onto me? No, they're not. Why would they be?" Paul sounded peevish and irritated, but his voice was higher in pitch and the trembling in his body was constant.

"Think about it. You staged your little lights out magic trick after the public reception was over. There was nobody but family and close friends there. How long did you think it would take for Lucas or Ryker or any of them to narrow the suspect field down to you?"

"The thief didn't have to be a friend or family member."

"Of course not. But the person who hired the thief did. Face it, Paul. They know it's you."

"Shut up and get on the floor!" Paul shouted.

To Cara Lynn's dismay, Jack shook his head. "You want me on the floor, you're going to have to put me there yourself. Or are you too much of a coward?"

"Jack," she said, her voice raspy with emotion. "Do it. He's out of control."

Paul stiffened and his face turned nearly purple. "You're treading on thin ice, Bush."

"Jack—!" Cara Lynn said. She was terrified. Jack

with his hands cuffed behind his back and Paul with a loaded handgun didn't equal a fair fight.

She was standing to Paul's right and slightly behind him. Jack was beyond her, facing Paul. At that angle, she could see Jack's shoulder and arm muscles tensing as he tried to manipulate the flex cuffs without Paul noticing. That's why he was taunting Paul. He was doing his best to keep Paul's attention on what he was saying and not what he was doing.

"Thin ice?" Jack laughed.

"Get on the floor!" Paul demanded, brandishing the gun. "Now!"

Just as Cara Lynn had made up her mind that she could rush Paul and knock the gun out of his hand, he glanced at her. "Get over here near Jack," he said, gesturing with the barrel of the gun, "so I can keep an eye on you."

Reluctantly, she moved. "What more can you possibly want? Just take the stuff and go. We'll count to three hundred. We'll count to three thousand. I swear. Just go."

He ignored her. "I'm giving you one more chance to get on the floor on your stomach, Jack."

Jack shrugged and with that movement, Cara Lynn saw the tie on his left hand slip up his wrist toward his thumb. "I'm good right here."

Paul raised his gun hand and lunged at Jack. He swung the gun's barrel at Jack's head. Jack twisted, but Paul connected anyway.

Cara Lynn saw blood spray into the air as if in slow motion. She watched the tiny red droplets hover for what seemed like seconds, before they fell. They sprayed across Paul's face and neck and several drops hit her.

Jack went down. Cara Lynn leaped toward him, crying his name. And Paul backhanded her. The gun didn't hit her but his forearm and elbow did and she fell against the kitchen table, then tumbled to the floor. She hit on her butt and her elbow, but the pain barely registered. She immediately righted herself and started crawling on her hands and knees toward Jack.

"Don't move, Cara Lynn," Paul said. He recovered his balance immediately and held the gun on her. "Don't!"

She froze, shuddering at the idea of the gun's barrel pointed straight at the top of her head. "Jack—?" she said.

At her words, Jack moved and groaned. He was on his side, his arms still behind his back. His face was smeared with blood, but when Cara Lynn looked closer, she saw that all the blood was coming from a cut on his chin.

He lifted his head, shook it, moaned, and let it drop.

Paul walked around him and approached him from the far side, so he could still keep Cara Lynn in his sights. "I told you not to mess with me, Broussard," he said and lifted his leg to kick Jack over onto his stomach.

At that point, for Cara Lynn, everything became a blur. She saw Jack whirl, saw more blood as his legs slammed into Paul's calves. Paul staggered as one leg went out from under him.

Jack's left hand came free and he used it to grab at

the gun as Paul hopped on one leg, trying to hold on to his balance. Jack used his right arm, from which the flex ties dangled to push himself into a crouch. He latched onto Paul's right wrist with his left arm and was doing his best to wrest or knock the gun from Paul's hand.

As Jack got his legs securely under him and vaulted upward, Paul swung his gun arm around toward Cara Lynn.

"Cara, down!" Jack cried.

She'd already seen the barrel of the gun point toward her and dove behind the kitchen table, covering her head with her hands. A gunshot rang out and something stung her on the arm. Then another shot exploded, then a third.

Then quiet. Cara Lynn's ears were ringing, but there were no more explosions. She dared to look up. Paul and Jack were rolling on the floor. Paul still had the gun, but Jack had both hands around Paul's wrist.

She watched, cringing every time the gun moved. But something wasn't quite right. The two of them must have been getting tired, because they were slowing down. A lot.

Then the gun fired again. She ducked, but she was apparently tired, too, because she was moving too slowly. Slow as molasses as her grandmother always said.

The bullet plowed a furrow in the table leg in front of her, and she toppled over onto the floor and lay there, wondering why she was so exhausted all of a sudden.

In her line of vision, Paul's ridiculously dyed hair and Jack's dark brown head bounced around and around. Then, just as Cara Lynn decided she was too tired to watch any more, another explosion filled the air, someone yelped in pain and something heavy thudded to the ground.

Cara Lynn closed her eyes. She couldn't remember why she'd thought it was so important to keep them open. Her last thought was that whatever kind of bee or wasp had stung her arm must have been huge.

CARA LYNN SQUINTED at what she figured had to be the sun. It was huge and bright. The only thing that wasn't sunlike about it was that it was long and skinny—kind of like a big fluorescent light, and it wasn't hot.

She opened her eyes to a narrow slit and suddenly the light was blocked by faces. She opened her eyes a little more and the faces started spinning, so she closed them again, really fast.

"Cara Lynn, it's your mom." She felt a soft, cool hand on her forehead. "Wake up, baby. Are you okay?"

She heard her mother's voice quiver. What was the problem and why were there so many people hovering over her? She lifted her hand to shade her eyes—or at least she tried to. It felt like her hand was tied down. She tried again and again, it wouldn't lift.

"Hold on, kiddo." A big, warm hand touched hers.

"Lucas?" she said, hearing how hoarse her voice was. "What's—?"

"Stay still, or the nurse will make us leave," Lucas said, patting her hand. "Everything's fine. You just ran into a little trouble. Mom, turn the overhead light out. I think it's bothering her eyes."

The world beyond her eyelids got a lot less bright.

"That better, Care-Care?" It was Harte.

Cara Lynn opened her eyes. They felt heavy and sticky, but after a few blinks she could see out of them. And she'd been right. There were a bunch of faces. Her whole family, it looked like. She focused on the most familiar of all the familiar faces. Her mother's. "Mom? What's going on?"

Her mother smiled down at her. "Cara Lynn, honey. We were so worried." Her mother's eyes filled with tears.

"What's going on?" she said, louder, and tried to push herself up in the—*bed*. It was a bed. A *hospital* bed.

"Hey, Cara Lynn," Christy said, leaning in and smiling at her. "Reilly, press that blue button down there. She wants to sit up." Christy put her hand on Cara Lynn's—the one that wouldn't move like she wanted it to.

"You're in the hospital," Christy said, patting her hand.

Cara Lynn nodded. That much she'd figured out.

"Your hand has an IV in it, just for a little while. You're okay. Your arm was nicked by a bullet and you hit your head. But you're doing fine. They bandaged your arm and we're just going to stay here overnight to make sure you don't have a concussion or any bleeding from that little bump. Okay?"

"Come on, Chris," Cara Lynn said, not quite as clearly as she'd have liked. "I know you're a pediatrician, but I'm an adult, okay?"

"Hey, Care-Care," Harte jumped in. "Be nice, okay? Christy's only trying to help."

Cara Lynn had only been awake for a couple of minutes, and she was already tired of her overprotective, suffocating family. She closed her eyes and turned her head away from Harte's voice. "Could everybody leave please?" she said. "I need to think—" her voice broke and she felt hot tears slipping down her cheeks.

She heard a cacophony of voices, all speaking at once. Her family. Her wonderful, irritating family.

"Hey!" she cried hoarsely, feeling a raw ache in her throat. "Please! Go!" The tears were falling harder now. "All but Christy."

The voices continued, but they began to fade as people left. Finally, she heard the door close with a quiet whoosh.

She sighed. "Chris?"

"Right here," Christy said. "Baby doctor, at your service." She sat on the edge of the bed near Cara Lynn's left hand.

"What's going—on?" Cara Lynn asked, still confused and wondering why she was suddenly sobbing.

"What do you remember?" Christy asked.

She shook her head. "Nothing. I—" but she did remember something. She remembered droplets of blood floating in the air. She remembered a sweet, secret smile that was just for her.

"Oh—oh my God, where's Jack? Is he okay?" She got her hands pressed into the plastic-covered mattress on the hospital bed and pushed herself up as much as she could. "Christy, do you know where he is?"

Christy held out a hand as if to make sure Cara Lynn didn't jump out of bed. "Shh. Hang on a minute. Everything's okay. Jack's okay. Paul is okay—mostly okay."

"Jack's okay? Are you sure? I saw a lot of blood. It was all Jack's," she said, her voice hoarse with emotion and drowsiness.

"Paul hit him on the chin with the gun barrel. He had four stitches in that beautiful face."

"Oh," Cara Lynn said, her eyes welling with tears that Jack had been hurt. Then she thought about Paul. "What happened to Paul?"

"He's in jail. Remanded because he's a flight risk. Reilly said he'll probably have to serve time for something. Claire's lawyers have found a bank account in his name in the Cayman Islands. Apparently there's something over a million dollars in it. And then he'll certainly be indicted for kidnapping, assault, attempted assault with a deadly weapon." Christy shook her head. "The list goes on. I kind of feel sorry for him."

Cara Lynn nodded. "I know," she said thoughtfully. "Me, too."

Christy looked up at the IV that was hanging from a pole, with clear tubing leading from it into the back of Cara Lynn's right hand. Cara Lynn could tell that she was calculating something.

"You checking to see how much morphine I've had—or Valium or whatever?" she asked. "I'm fine. I can take it. Tell me what happened. Is Jack really okay?"

Christy raised her eyebrows and pinned Cara Lynn with a look. "I'm not going to tell you a thing until you calm down. I might have to report to your physician that you're having symptoms of brain trauma."

Cara Lynn laughed, but Christy looked completely sincere. She cleared her throat, which was feeling even more sore. "What is wrong with my throat?" she asked.

"When they went in to get the bullet out of your arm, they intubated you."

"Intub—why?" Cara Lynn looked at her arm which was bandaged. "The bullet was still in there?"

"Not deep, but it was."

"Okay. Can you just fill in the blanks for me?"

Just as she finished speaking there was a knock on the door. Christy raised a finger in the air, then stepped to the door and peeked out. When she turned around there was an enigmatic smile on her face. "I think there's someone here who can answer your questions better than I can. I'm just going to slip out now. Why don't you buzz the nurse's station when you feel like you're ready for visitors, or ready to go to sleep." Christy's smile grew larger. "Either one is okay. I'll send the family home if that's what you want." Then she disappeared, pulling the door closed behind her.

Cara Lynn called out, "Christy—wait!"

The door opened to a crack, but it faced the wrong direction for Cara Lynn to be able to get a peek at who was there. "Christy?" she called.

No answer.

"Mom?"

Then the door opened wider and a dark figure stepped into the room. It took Cara Lynn a moment to focus on the battered face, and another moment for her to recognize it.

"Jack," she breathed. "Oh—"

He was in the slacks and polo shirt he'd been in when he'd come into their apartment to confront Paul. Both the slacks and the shirt were streaked with blood. His hair was mussed and tousled, and his chin was red and purple and swollen and had a strip bandage on it.

"Oh, Jack—are you all—right?" she said, between sobs. "I saw a—lot of bl-blood."

He moved a few steps closer. His eyes were dark as black holes, but that sweet smile was still on his face. Although it looked to her like it was wavering. "Hey, Cara. I'm fine. The question is—how are you?" He looked down at his feet, then back up. "I didn't know you'd been shot."

"Me, either," she said.

His smile faded. "I'm sorry. I'm so sorry for everything that happened." He looked down at the floor again, then at a place somewhere to the left of her eyes. His face was serious now, no trace of that beautiful smile. "I screwed things up so badly."

She pushed herself up in the bed again. "These damn sheets are slippery," she said, then held out her free hand. Jack stepped closer and took it in his. "You didn't screw up," she said, then gave him a small smile. "At least not everything."

"Cara, hon, can you—" he stopped. He looked at her and raised his chin slightly, as if readying himself for a blow. He cleared his throat. "Could you—would you—marry me?"

She stared at him in shock. "Jack? We—we are married." Then she narrowed her gaze. "Aren't we?"

He sat down on the bed, still holding her hand, looking down at it. "I just want it to be for the right reasons this time," he said softly.

She smiled at him and shook her head. "I'll be happy to marry you again, for the right reasons. Just don't tell my mother, or we'll have to do the big North Shore wedding."

"Well," he said, playing with the ring on her left ring finger. "I sort of already did," he said without looking up. "So we have to do the North Shore wedding now."

She pulled her hand away from his grasp and reached out to cradle his cheek in her palm.

He raised his gaze to hers.

She sighed and shook her head. "Why did you tell her?" she whispered.

"Why? To get in good with her of course," he said. "By the way, she wants you to wear her wedding dress, although according to the doctors, you'll have to get it let out."

"Let out? What are you talking about?" Behind Jack, the hospital door opened and her whole family flowed into the room, acting as though they were trying to be quiet and unobtrusive, but every single one of them had a huge grin on his or her face, and giggles and chuckles kept erupting.

Jack leaned forward and kissed her gently, then pulled away until he could gaze into her eyes. "Apparently, you're pregnant."

"I'm—what?"

He nodded. "About four weeks." He smiled, but his eyes looked wary. "Cara, I love you," he said. "Kiss me?"

"I'm pregnant?" Cara Lynn felt stunned. "And—and you *want* to kiss me?"

"When we kiss, I find myself wanting to confess everything to you. It made it really hard to lie to you."

Cara Lynn's grin broadened, and behind Jack, her family was grinning and beaming as well.

"Then we will definitely be kissing a *lot*," she declared. She lifted her good hand. "Everybody, come in. Apparently there are going to be two babies coming soon!"

As Cara Lynn's family gathered around the bed, all talking and smiling, Jack felt something he had never felt before. He understood, for the first time, what it meant to be part of a family. He'd had a mother and for a short time, a father. And of course his grandfather, his Papi, had been his family. But this was a lot different. The Delancey clan was dozens of people, who seemed to be accepting him into their large extended family.

It was kind of strange, but it also warmed a place inside him that had never been warm before.

"Jacques," Cara Lynn said, laughing. *"Je t'aime."*

Jack kissed her—on the mouth.

Epilogue

Several weeks later, Jack and Cara Lynn walked out of the courtroom. Harte Delancey walked with them.

"I don't understand," Jack said, cringing inside. "None of the rest of the family wanted to be here? Was it just too hard for them?"

Harte smiled as he shook his head. "Not at all. We all agreed that I'd come, just because I represent the entire family, and the media would be out in droves if a dozen or more Delanceys showed up.

"But every one of them is happy that the truth has finally come out and justice has been served," Cara Lynn added.

Jack opened the passenger-side door for her and watched as she got in. Her baby bump was barely visible, but she was more beautiful than ever. He would swear in a court of law that she had an ethereal glow that he knew had to come from carrying her precious cargo. As he closed the door, she reached for her seat belt.

When he turned, Harte was standing there with his

hand extended. "Congratulations, Jack. Armand Brous-sard has been cleared of all charges related to the death of Con Delancey."

Jack couldn't help but smile. "Thanks," he said, then sobered. "But are you sure the family is okay with this?"

Harte shrugged. "All I can say is that Mom is having a cookout this afternoon and I'm scheduled to cook the steaks. The whole clan is planning to come. Even Hannah and Mack."

Cara Lynn, who had let the passenger window down, chimed in. "Let's go. I'm starving," she said. "I need protein."

Jack looked at her and then back at Harte. Finally, he nodded. "Okay. Let's go get this pregnant woman some protein."

Harte cleared his throat. When Jack turned, Cara Lynn's brother's face was bright red.

Behind him, she said, "Harte? What is it?"

"Well," he said, his mouth spreading into a huge grin. "It looks like there are three, not just two pregnant Delancey women."

"Harte!" Cara Lynn cried, opening the car door and jumping out to hug her brother.

Jack put an arm around Harte's shoulder and gave him a quick hug, too.

"Dani's pregnant? That's *wonderful!*" Cara Lynn said as tears streamed down her face. "Oh, no! Everything makes me cry these days."

Jack let go of Harte and took Cara Lynn in his arms.

"I think you're gorgeous when you cry. Let's go," he said, sending Harte a congratulatory nod over Cara's shoulder. "The family's waiting for us."

* * * * *